Faelorehn

A Novella of the Otherworld

by
Jenna Elizabeth Johnson

Copyrighted Material

This is a work of fiction. Names, characters and incidents are a product of the author's imagination. All material in connection with Celtic myth has been borrowed and interpreted for use in the plot of the story only. Cover image is the sole property of the author. The *Faelorehn* font on the cover image and interior of this book was created by P.A. Vannucci (www.alphabetype.it) to be used in the Otherworld Trilogy. Any resemblance to actual persons is entirely coincidental.

Ehriad

Copyright © 2013 by Jenna Elizabeth Johnson
All rights reserved.
No part of this book or its cover may be reproduced in any manner without written permission from its creator.
For more information and to contact the author, visit:
www.jennaelizabethjohnson.com

Contents

A Single Thread of Magic
-1-

The Morrigan's Game
-31-

Broken Geis
-54-

Ehriad

A Single Thread of Magic

The sharp snap of a twig and a low, almost imperceptible growl informed me that the creature I hunted was now only a few yards away. I assumed his snarl of frustration was aimed towards the branch he'd broken, giving away his presence, and not by any means meant to intimidate me. No matter. I had planned it this way. I had known he'd been following me for a good fifteen minutes now. It helped when you had another pair of eyes, and a good nose, to lend a hand.

How close? I sent to my spirit guide.

Ten feet, to the right, Fergus answered.

His mind was sharp; focused on the hunt. Even better.

I let my body ease out of the tense stance it had taken at hearing the sound of the snapped twig. *One more minute Fergus.* I'd let the creature stalk me for sixty seconds more.

The thing about faelah is despite their vicious, blood-thirsty tendencies, they aren't very smart. I was only a few feet from the dolmarehn now, boxed in on most sides by the steep walls of the culvert, and the faelah was somewhere above me, close to the edge but remaining out of sight.

What exactly are we dealing with? I asked my spirit guide.

About my size, dark, no hair. Small eyes, big teeth, sharp, thin claws and a tail like a rat.

Ebrial

I nodded to myself. This particular monster resembled most other faelah: the grotesque, zombie-like imitations of animals created from the long-dead body parts of many others. If the people of the mortal world could see it, they would be cursed with a lifetime of nightmares to disrupt their sleep.

Fortunately for them, the faelah's glamour kept it invisible from sight. No, only my people, the Faelorehn, could see the faelah. At least until they were destroyed and a small window between the time their glamour faded from their bodies and their flesh turned to ash did the mere mortals get a chance to catch a glimpse. This was one of the main reasons I lured as many as I could back into the Otherworld, or at least deep enough into the woods to kill them where they wouldn't be seen by anyone.

The crunch of dead leaves met my ears again, along with Fergus's words: *Get ready.*

I slipped my hand into my boot, pulling out a long knife, pressing the dull side against my forearm so that I could stab if necessary.

In the next breath, the faelah leapt from the edge of the ravine and used the trunks of dead trees crisscrossing my path like ladder rungs to make its way down. The faelah came to rest only fifteen feet in front of me, a monster looking very much like a partially decomposed mountain lion. It growled at me, showing several long teeth, and twitched its reedy tail. Just as I had suspected, this one wasn't going to let me lead it back into the Otherworld. Looks like it would have to be a kill. Not that I regretted it much. Most of the faelah had been alive at one time, but not anymore, not really. I bared my teeth in a grimace, hoping to intimidate the beast.

A flash of white caught the corner of my eye and a giant wolfhound joined us, using the same method the faelah had to reach the gully floor. He landed behind the creature, bearing his teeth and laying his rusty ears flat against his skull.

Kill? he sent to me.

A Single Thread of Magic

Yes, this one will have to be a kill. The beast howled and snapped its jaws before hunkering down on its hindquarters.

Here goes . . .

With preternatural speed the faelah leapt, mouth gaping open, massive paws tipped with needle-thin claws outstretched. I froze for a fraction of a second, then with one swift movement, jerked my hand diagonally across my body, swiping the sharp edge of my blade against leathery skin.

The yowl in the monster's throat died and I quickly sidestepped, letting the body hurtle past me. It landed in a tangled heap in the dirt, the head nearly severed from the rest of the body. Its limbs twitched a few times as black, putrid blood spilled from the open wound. I wrinkled my nose at the smell, but didn't gag. I was used to the stench.

As I cleaned my blade I felt the faelah's glamour swell like a bubble, growing larger and larger until it burst. There was nothing to see really, but my own well of magic felt it all the same. If there had been mortals around, they would now be gaping, dumbfounded at the atrocity lying at their feet. I didn't even stay to make sure it turned to dust.

"Come on Fergus, time to go," I said to the wolfhound.

Wounds? he sent to me.

No, not even a scratch. I was, after all, very good at my job.

We hiked out of the woods and through the small swamp that rested behind a sparse neighborhood. I often patrolled this area because my home resided just on the other side of the dolmarehn hidden at the end of the ravine. I longed to head home, back to Eilé, but I needed to return my car to the small garage I used as storage when spending any extended amount of time in the mortal world.

I crossed over the lowest part of the swamp and headed up the trail that veered off from the one the local horse owners often used. Five minutes later I found my car, a classic black Trans Am complete with a silver Phoenix emblem emblazoned on the hood. I grinned. I

Ehriad

wasn't a big fan of the machinery and technology of the mortal world, but I had a soft spot for this car. As I approached, I ran my hand along the hood, petting it as if it were a dog.

Fergus snorted next to me and I gave him a look over my shoulder. He returned it with a canine grin, his tongue falling out of his mouth in a pant.

"We all have our indulgences, Fergus," I murmured, smiling as I dug the keys out of my trench coat pocket.

Teaching myself how to drive had been quite an adventure, and I had to be careful because being from the Otherworld the only driver's license I owned was a fake one. This was the main reason I never took the Trans Am out to test its racing capabilities; couldn't risk getting pulled over and questioned.

I unlocked the door and swung it open, but before I so much as set a single foot into the car, something familiar brushed against my senses. My well of glamour flared and I drew in a sharp breath, clutching a hand to the middle of my chest.

What in Eilé . . . ?

I shot a look at Fergus, but he only back-stepped a few paces and whined.

My breath was coming in short bursts and it took a while for the sensation to burn off. It wasn't unpleasant really, just unexpected. I glanced up and gazed down into the small valley dominated by the acres of eucalyptus trees and swampland. That burst of sensation hadn't come from any faelah I'd ever encountered, and I've encountered more than most. Yet, it had felt so familiar.

I shook my head to get rid of the feeling, gritting my teeth as I sunk into the driver's seat of my car. I gripped the steering wheel until my knuckles showed white; until the feeling faded away and my heartbeat returned to normal. Fergus whined again and I leaned over to open the passenger side door for him.

I turned the key in the ignition and the car rumbled to life. As I pulled onto the highway, my mind was completely occupied with the

A Single Thread of Magic

small burst of power that had slammed into my own glamour like a raging bull. What was it, and would I be able to find its source? Taking a deep breath, I made a mental note to seek it out the next time I was in the swamp.

The wheels of the Trans Am crunched over gravel and the rumble of the engine set the dogs in the junkyard beside my place into a fit of barking. I hit the button to open the garage door and glided in onto smooth concrete. I had purchased this small place several years ago, when it became apparent that the faelah wouldn't stop visiting this particular area on the Central Coast. It wasn't much: a garage large enough to fit my car with a studio above it. I didn't stay here more than a few days at a time, but it served well as my headquarters when I needed to track down renegade Otherworldly monsters.

Before closing the garage door, I stepped out onto the asphalt and scooped up the newspapers from the past several days. I had been gone a week in the Otherworld and now I needed to check the headlines for any 'strange sightings' while I was away. Humans couldn't see faelah because of their glamour, but sometimes the little beasts stayed longer in the mortal world than they should and that glamour started to fade away. Any time I picked up the paper and read reports of odd things happening, I knew there were some Otherworldly creatures that had to be dealt with. I didn't particularly enjoy my job, but because of the geis, or curse, set upon me several years ago in Eilé, I was now Ehríad, a faelah bounty hunter with no true connections to anyone. My occupation was simple, really: I would enter the mortal world and round up anything Otherworldly. Then I would either send it back to where it came from or destroy it if it proved difficult, like the creature today.

Fergus barked at me as I re-entered the garage, carrying several rolls of newspaper with me. I opened the door and let him out just before hitting the button to close the garage door. My place wasn't in the best part of town, but it suited my purposes. The neighbors on one side ran a welding shop and those on the other, a wrecking yard. Let's just say it was seldom quiet. Luckily, this wasn't my permanent home.

Whistling to Fergus, I jogged up the stairs and the single room studio greeted me in its usual fashion. A couch hiding a fold out bed, a small kitchen, a bathroom with a shower, and a single, broad window that looked out over the street and the storage center beyond it.

I walked over to an old beat up desk and threw the newspapers on top, then stepped towards the tiny kitchen. Hunting down deadly faelah had a way of working up one's appetite. I checked Fergus's bowl and quickly poured in some dog food as I pulled out a frozen dinner from the freezer. Fergus sniffed at the food and huffed.

I glanced at the frozen dinner and nearly mimicked him.

"I know, but we won't be going back to Eilé until tomorrow, so you had best eat it."

A half an hour later we were both enjoying the mortal world's food to the best of our abilities. I poured myself a glass of water and sat down at the desk, flipping open a laptop, my latest investment. Yes, I wasn't a fan of technology, but having a computer in the mortal world was more useful than having an umbrella in the rain. I opened a file from my desktop and a detailed map of the area took up the screen. I scanned it, taking note of all the dolmarehn I knew of. Only the one in the swamp was big enough for someone my size to fit through. The rest were small. And that is where the problem lay. The faelah normally didn't sneak through the big dolmarehn because I kept a pretty close eye on it, but when the entire Central Coast area was riddled with smaller portals to the Otherworld, then someone had to visit this world every now and again to keep the vermin under control. For some reason, faelah enjoyed hunting in this world more than their own, and more often than not, they grew accustomed to the taste of small rodents and house pets.

A Single Thread of Magic

Sighing, I flipped through the newspapers, searching the pages for anything out of the ordinary. Local pets gone missing, coyotes suspected . . . Okay, that might be a lead. I scanned the paragraphs. Nope. No remains ever found. Coyotes often ate most of what they caught. Keep reading. Burglaries, aggravated assault, a string of car thefts . . .

My eyes skidded to a halt when I turned the page. The headline read: *Chupacabra Sighting in Santa Maria.* Bingo. I read the first few lines of the article and felt my mouth tugging into a small smile. Horrendous looking creature, puncture wounds in the necks of the cattle, attacked at night . . . Yes, all the signs pointed towards something Otherworldly. I took note of the location, Costa Robles Ranch, and searched the internet for directions. I shut down the computer and went to take a shower. When I came out ten minutes later, I found Fergus lying on the couch. He perked his rusty ears forward and cocked his head to the side.

"Off the couch Fergus. We need to get some rest if we're to go out hunting tonight."

Fergus jumped off the couch so I could pull out the bed. Five minutes later I had my arm flung over my eyes as I tried to block out the crashing of metal in the junkyard and the familiar crack-pop of welding next door. Despite the noise and the light streaming through the cracks in the blinds, I managed to doze off into a half sleep.

Sneaking onto the ranch was not an issue. Located just north of the Santa Maria River and just off the main highway, the Costa Robles Ranch covered several acres of rolling land scattered with oak trees and the occasional dry gully cutting between the hills. I wasn't too worried about being spotted since it was, after all, the middle of the night. The moon provided just enough light to see by, and what I couldn't detect myself Fergus helped with his canine senses.

Ebriad

I pulled my car off the highway and onto a side road, killing the engine and turning off the lights. Fergus and I climbed through a heavy ranch-style gate and began our trek across the fields. I moved as silently as the broken earth would allow, trying not to startle the cattle I could sense dozing in the distance, their black shapes barely standing out against the pale moonlight. Fergus loped ahead of me, disappearing over the hilltop crowned with a copse of oak trees.

Death, he sent.

A chill ran down my spine. *How fresh?*

Very.

I gritted my teeth and crouched even lower, but kept my forward movement smooth. The odor of cow dung and dried grass was soon obliterated by the sharp metallic scent of hot blood. I maneuvered through the low oaks, drawing my broadsword from its sheath on my back. In the daylight, I'd be comfortable with my single edged blade, but in the darkness I needed something larger; something a little more lethal. When eliminating faelah, hawthorn worked the best, but any weapon forged in the Otherworld would also do the job. A white shape appearing against the darkness and a low growl informed me that I'd found Fergus. I wrinkled my nose as the smell of blood grew stronger.

In front of us lay a calf, the dark stains on its pale hide all that remained of its blood. Wonderful. A bloodsucking faelah. Those were the worst kind of Otherworldly aberrations because they let their desire for blood rule them. No fear, no caution. If you were warm and full of blood, then you might as well be a walking all-you-can-eat buffet.

The sharp cry of cattle and a low hiss drew my attention from the dead calf.

Fergus growled more loudly, his hackles rising along the ridge of his spine.

Twenty feet. Faelah draining one of the herd.

Go around wide, I sent back to my spirit guide, *there may be more than one.*

A Single Thread of Magic

I lifted my sword into a front guard, not wanting to be unprepared in case the monster lost interest in the cattle.

The herd slept in a small clearing, the moon shedding just enough light for me to see that something wasn't right about the cow closest to me. An odd shape protruded from behind its neck. The shape moved, like a snake striking, and the cow bellowed out a sound of pain before falling onto its knees. No more time to hesitate. I swept my sword wide, bringing the blade down, biting into the back of the faelah. The creature squealed in pain, but it had been too distracted by its warm meal to realize I was there.

The creature slumped off the dying cow and I kicked it with my foot so that it landed in a patch of moonlight. About the size of a fox, it had a round head with large, bat-like ears and a nose like a pug. Short forearms ended with three fingers tipped with long, sharp claws. The hind legs were a different story. They'd be several feet long if fully extended. This thing was meant for jumping. A hide resembling that of a dried up frog and a short, hairless tail completed the grotesque ensemble.

Letting out a breath I hadn't realized I was holding, I used the tip of my sword to peel back the thing's lips. I blanched. Four long, wicked canines crowded out the other teeth in the front of its jaw.

Fergus whimpered behind me. *There are more!*

Before I had a chance to turn back around, something hit me with enough force to knock the air from my lungs. Unfortunately, whatever it was also clung to me like a leech. I tried to gain my balance and shake it off, but the cloak I had decided to wear for this hunt only tangled with the monster and gave it something to hang on to.

Finally, I got my feet under me, but in the next second a sharp pain ripped through the muscles of my shoulder. I shouted in anger and agony, trying my best to shake the faelah off. Fergus was barking like mad, snapping and growling at what I could only assume were more monsters. My attacker was too close and I couldn't get my sword around to cause any damage.

Ebriad

I panted and reached down for my dagger. The faelah dug its teeth and claws in deeper, and it took all my strength to keep from blacking out. The glamour that rested beside my heart flared, bearing its own teeth as it demanded to be set free. No . . . no I couldn't let it out. This was another part of me, one I kept hidden unless all other options failed. If I let it break free, I would lose all control and might not have the strength to return to my car once this was over . . .

Grinding my teeth together, I fought the pain in my shoulder and the angry demand of my power. I worked my dagger free and brought it up, slipping it under the ribs of the faelah and driving it directly into its heart. The creature released its hold and gave a guttural gasp before falling to the ground.

Fetid blood stained my shirt and cloak, but I bit back the pain and turned to see how Fergus fared. The shadows of the night hindered my view, but I was able to count three more faelah still moving. Fergus had killed two, and I one, not including the first one.

Kill? Fergus asked, his teeth bared as he panted.

Yes, I sent, my sight almost going red with fury. *All of them.*

The final three faelah were easy to dispatch, now that I didn't have one clinging to me and turning my arm into mincemeat. I waited until all the bodies turned to ash, then sent Fergus to scout for any more we might have missed. By the time we returned to the car, the eastern horizon was awash in the pale turquoise of dawn.

Three times I almost fell asleep on the way home, Fergus barking every now and then to keep me awake. The fight had taken far more than I expected and despite the need to see to my wounds and the desire for another shower, I parked in my garage and started out across the highway. Thank goodness the swamp was only a thirty minute walk away. Fergus trotted ahead of me, checking for cars and other obstacles. My glamour was dangerously low and I was beginning to suspect that the chupacabra-like faelah might have been venomous.

The air was cold and damp and grew even more so as I descended into the swamp. When I took the first step into the culvert

A Single Thread of Magic

that housed the dolmarehn, I stumbled. I gritted my teeth and clutched at my shoulder, fighting the waves of pain that threatened to overtake me. Beads of sweat formed on my forehead and my knees felt like rubber. This wasn't good.

"Just a few more steps Fergus." My voice didn't sound like it belonged to me. It was dry and raspy and it hurt my throat to speak.

Fergus yipped.

They didn't bite you too, did they? I sent.

No. Tried, though.

I nodded. Even that hurt.

The dead trunks of eucalyptus trees crisscrossed the gorge ahead of me and I let out a shuddering breath. Not much further. Crossing between them took more effort than it should have, and just when I thought my legs wouldn't carry me another step, I spotted the cave entrance. I collapsed to my knees just inside and exhaustion overtook me.

Fergus whined again and I felt something tugging on the hood of my cloak.

Twenty feet, he sent. *Rest when in Eilé.*

I didn't want to move twenty feet; such a distance seemed too far, but Fergus wouldn't stop tugging on my cloak. And this was my good cloak. Didn't want him to tear it. Groaning, I dragged myself up onto my hands and knees and crawled deeper into the cave. I didn't dare stop until I felt the familiar tug of the Otherworld's magic. After that, I gave in to the fatigue and lost consciousness before reaching the other side.

❄ ❄ ❄

I woke up to the sensation of Fergus licking my face. Grumbling, I shoved him away with my left arm, sighing in relief when I registered no pain. I blinked several times, removing the sleep from my eyes, and caught a glimpse of oak trees layered in moss, a gray sky and several stone monoliths gazing down on me.

I sat up, scratching Fergus on the head to let him know I appreciated his loyalty and slowly removed my cloak and shirt. The misty air of Eilé was cold against my bare skin, but I had to make sure my wounds had healed. I ran a hand over my shoulder, feeling the small knots of new scarring, but no festering wounds. My arm proved to be in the same condition. I shrugged my shirt back on, frowning at the tears and bloodstains. Oh well. Perks of the job. One couldn't complain when they had the magic of the Otherworld to revive them.

I stood and stretched the stiffness away, yawning and running my fingers through my hair. It was slightly tangled and disheveled, but that didn't surprise me.

"How long was I out?" I asked my spirit guide.

He panted and flicked his ears forward. *Three days.*

I winced. Those bloodsucking faelah must have been more venomous than I had thought.

"I guess we'd better head back. There's no telling how many faelah have crept over into the mortal world while I've been napping."

Fergus yipped, as if to tell me I thought too highly of my own importance. I shot him a wry grin and turned towards the cave that was framed with the stones of the dolmarehn.

The next several weeks passed this way, with Fergus and I darting back and forth between the mortal world and the Otherworld. Every now and then, after tracking a faelah and either killing it or herding it back into Eilé, I would detect a tiny hint of the strange magic that had overwhelmed me the day I destroyed the bloodsucking faelah. And every time, the magic would fade away into nothing and I'd be left grasping at straws.

A Single Thread of Magic

One autumn morning as Fergus and I were hiking up the equestrian trail behind the swamp, an invisible stream of power slammed into me. I stopped dead and shook my head, leaning over and resting my hands on my knees. What in the world . . . ? My own glamour flared in response. I rubbed at the spot on my chest and took a few deep breaths. It was the same strange yet familiar magic I'd felt those several weeks ago, but fresher. Where was it coming from? I had to find out.

Being what I was, being Ehríad, meant that it was my responsibility to keep tabs on anything Otherworldly that existed on this side of the dolmarehn, faelah or not. An idea came to me and I closed my eyes. Perhaps if I simply felt for the magic . . . In my mind's eye I saw a faint, crooked string of pale turquoise blue twining off into the distance above the horse path leading to one of the neighborhoods.

Fergus whined softly next to me.

"Hold on Fergus, I've found a trail of weak glamour," I murmured, my eyes still closed.

I breathed in deeply through my nose, drawing on a small amount of my own power, pushing and pulling it into a shell that would erase me from view. Opening my eyes, I left the path running to the road and followed the thread of magic instead. Fifteen minutes later I stumbled upon a house perched at the edge of a small hill overlooking the swamp. The yard backed up into the woods and small spots of vibrant blue glamour pooled around it.

"It's as if something from the Otherworld has sprung a leak," I mused.

At that very moment, a door slammed shut and someone walked from the house. I stayed put, relying on my magic to keep me hidden. I couldn't see the girl very well; she wore a light jacket with the hood pulled over her head, but she carried a backpack and looked too old for middle school.

I should have turned around then and gone back to my apartment. I could have written down the address and looked the girl up later on the internet from the safety of my garage, but I felt compelled to follow her, if just for a few minutes.

Fergus, hide yourself with glamour. We're following the girl.

The white wolfhound obeyed without a sound and we continued silently up the path, staying several feet behind her. I may have been invisible, but I could still scrape my boots against the asphalt and give away my presence, so I used the distance to help hide any sounds I made. As I walked, I shut my eyes for a split second and noted the ribbon of blue unfurling behind her. So, the glamour was coming from her, but how? Perhaps she'd had an encounter with some faelah or carried an object from the Otherworld.

I gritted my teeth. I didn't like the idea of following her around. It was intrusive and it went against my personal honor to be intrusive, but I also had to know where the glamour was coming from. It was never a good idea for Otherworldly and mortal things to mix.

Once at the end of the street, the girl stopped and chatted with another girl her age. I heard them say something about a high school, one I knew was only a few miles away. Before turning to leave them in peace, I picked up on the shorter, blond girl calling the other girl Meghan. So, I had a first name now. Breathing a sigh of relief, I turned around and headed back down the street. When I reached the end of the road, and before disappearing down into the swamp, I glanced back up at the house the girl had come out of. Above the front door was a carved wooden sign that read *The Elams*.

So, miss Meghan Elam, I won't have to work too hard to discern your identity after all.

Shaking my head, I tried to dispel the knot of guilt that was growing in my stomach. I didn't make it a habit to stalk young women, but when someone was so obviously shrouded in Otherworldly magic, I couldn't just ignore it.

Pushing the uneasy feelings aside, I continued on, seeking the path I knew would lead to the high school. The faelah had mostly stayed put in Eilé this week, and whether I wanted to or not, I needed

A Single Thread of Magic

to learn more about this girl with a string of blue, Otherworldly magic trailing after her.

* * *

I reached the outskirts of the high school within fifteen minutes of leaving behind the swamp. As I caught my breath, I studied the students pulling into the parking lot and reluctantly spilling out of their cars. I shied away from the barrage of smells and sounds that attacked my senses. Several dozen perfumes and colognes clouded the air, along with the high-pitched laughter and false promises being thrown from one person to the other. Combine that all together with the general angst and unavoidable desperation that permeated the atmosphere and it was enough to give one a headache. I was very glad I never had to attend high school in the Otherworld. I would not have survived it.

Fergus and I had been in this area only a week or so ago, checking into a possible faelah problem. I'd been wearing my old trench coat and had used my glamour to adopt the guise of an elderly homeless man. Most people left me alone when I took up that particular costume, so I wore the same cloak of glamour now: one of a decrepit, retired veteran down on his luck, lingering in the woods for no apparent reason.

A few more minutes ticked by before I caught a glimpse of that brilliant blue magic again. It trickled out of a gold minivan. I felt my muscles tense as the van pulled up and parked. The door rolled open and the girl, Meghan, stepped out with her friend. I took a small moment to wonder why I hadn't detected her strange magic here last week, but then brushed that thought aside once she started moving across the parking lot.

I focused my attention on the group of teenagers, especially the girl I had discovered earlier that morning. They were a good distance away, so I sacrificed a fraction of my glamour, pulling it away from my disguise and using it to enhance my vision just enough to get a clear picture of my quarry. The girl turned and looked in my direction. My relaxed pose stiffened. Pretty little thing, but not in a typically human way. In fact, I wouldn't be surprised if her peers thought her to be strange-looking. Humans were often a bad judge of real beauty, in my experience.

I continued to study her, grateful my hood covered most of my face. She was tall with dark, curling brown hair and high cheek bones, but it was her striking eyes that gave me pause. Hazel, flashing to gray, then green and blue, and back to hazel. My heart sped up and I felt my own well of power begin to burn, like a coal coaxed to life by a bellows. Not just a human tainted by glamour. Oh no, this girl was Faelorehn. Suddenly I felt winded, as if someone had punched me in the stomach.

There were plenty of Faelorehn and half-Faelorehn people living in the mortal world. Some chose to live here, some merely liked to visit. But there was something different about her; something I couldn't quite place. Most Faelorehn wore their glamour like a mantle, hiding their true identity in the mortal world. But this girl . . . Hers was locked away and almost impossible to see, like something lurking beneath a sheet of dark water. Yet the magic that trickled off of her was as visible as the stars in a moonless night sky.

The girl and her companions glanced away and I took the opportunity to slip behind the trees. I would look into who this girl was, this Faelorehn with hidden glamour. And while I was at it, I'd try to forget those eyes and her alluring face, too.

I visited the high school the next day to catch another glimpse of Meghan, just to make sure she was real, but the following day I had to return to Eilé. The Otherworld greeted me with the cool caress of fog and ancient magic. I sighed, shivering a little as the sensation poured over me. The mortal world's magic was much more subtle than

A Single Thread of Magic

this; much more concealed and gentle. The glamour of Eilé took hold of your senses and demanded that you pay attention, and if you chose to ignore it then more likely than not, that same magic would find a way to make you pay attention, and usually not in a pleasant way. Fortunately for me, I had lived a very long time in my homeland and I knew how to show respect to its raw, natural power.

Fergus and I traveled from the dolmarehn through the wooded hills, past the collection of ponds dotting the rolling fields, and on to Luathara, the castle that was left in my care. It more closely resembled a ruined pile of old stones than anything else, but there were a few rooms that were habitable with working fireplaces. The largest room on the third floor was where I often slept. It had a comfortable bed and a full-functioning bathroom (not a rarity in Eilé, but definitely an uncommon luxury at Luathara). I had dreams of one day returning the castle to its former glory; of settling down, to some extent, if I ever found a way to break free of the Morrigan's geis. As I thought about making a life at the castle, for some odd reason Meghan Elam's image flashed through my mind.

I stopped, just as my foot was about to hit the first step leading up to my rooms. Oh no. I shook my head. *None of that now Cade,* I told myself. Currently, I couldn't risk the luxury of thinking about young women in that way, and I most definitely couldn't think of the young Faelorehn girl I'd discovered hiding in the mortal world, either. First of all, she was too young for me and secondly, I knew nothing about her.

You know some things, my annoying conscience crooned. *She is very pretty, and she has strong magic, like yours . . .*

I growled and continued my progress upstairs. I would not think about Meghan Elam, and not only because it was a bad idea for my own sake, but for her sake as well.

"Stay here Fergus," I threw over my shoulder at the white wolfhound who followed me like a shadow. "I'm going to see the Morrigan."

Ehriad

My spirit guide whined softly and paused, watching me as I strode past my rooms and through the great gaping hole in the castle wall. I crossed the patio on the other side, my coat growing damp from the spray of the waterfall to my left. I took the stairs at the end of the terrace and descended into the caves that housed the dolmarehn to every imaginable destination in Eilé. I could take one to the edge of the Weald to visit Enorah, my sister, or I could take one that would bring me to the other side of my foster father's abode. But no, today I had to travel to the Morrigan's realm. My geis required that I check in with her once a month. And that was another reason why I had to stop thinking about Meghan, because if the Morrigan found out about her, her life might as well be over.

Eilé was a very large place, and many Faelorehn would tell you that it had no boundaries. They would also tell you that Erintara, the city of our high queen, was located in the exact center of our world. All the old kings and queens, the gods and goddesses of the ancient Celts, had their own realms, or large expanses of land they considered their own. The Morrigan's dominion was located on the easternmost stretch of land that nestled up against the endless mountains just on the other side.

I stepped through the dolmarehn and all of my muscles immediately seized up. The air was so frigid here it felt like a layer of ice coated my lungs every time I drew breath. I had walked out of another cave and into a small, rocky canyon devoid of anything living. The stones and skeletal trees that surrounded me reminded me of the bones of the dead. I gritted my teeth and made my way towards the mouth of the culvert where there stood a crude stone circle. Beyond that circle was a diseased forest full of dying trees, and even further past that were miles upon miles of desolate land littered with stones and

A Single Thread of Magic

shallow bogs. The Morrigan's kingdom was a place of death and despair.

I had been hanging my head as I walked, the sadness of this place acting like a weight to pull me down, but as I came upon the clearing and the stone circle, I glanced up and winced. She was waiting for me, the Morrigan, standing utterly still and wearing a dark blood-red cloak with the hood drawn over her head. An entourage of ravens sat scattered in the bare branches of a dead tree just behind her, watching me with baleful eyes. A pair of Cúmorrig, the Morrigan's personal hellhounds, stood by her side, their rotting flesh and putrescence making me gag.

As I closed the distance between us, she lowered her hood and crossed her arms casually. Though she stood more than a foot shorter than me, the very sight of her made my blood turn cold. Beautiful, like all the Faelorehn, with pale skin, black wavy hair and eyes that flashed red to reveal her powerful fae magic, the Morrigan was the most terrifying and dangerous person you could meet in Eilé. Her only desire was to cause war and strife and gain immeasurable power. Therefore, she had no concern for the feelings or well-being of others.

"Have my pets been misbehaving?" she asked in her seductive voice.

"Yes," I said shortly.

She sighed and rolled her eyes to a gray sky that threatened snow.

"How many did you have to destroy this time?"

I did a mental count in my head. "In the last month I've killed around thirty faelah."

She sneered, but didn't look too terribly disturbed by this information. "Such stupid little creatures. I wish I knew a way to make them more intelligent. It tires me to have to replace them all the time."

My jaw clenched at her callous tone of voice. It may tire her to construct her obscene creatures, but it cost others far more than that.

Ehriad

In order to bring her dead creations back to life, she needed the living essence of innocent victims, sometimes animal, sometimes Faelorehn.

Before I could help myself, I bit out, "Then stop making them."

She arched a perfect brow at me, her face blank with surprise, then her lips curled into a smile and she laughed.

"Oh Caedehn! You are so silly sometimes. After all these long years it still bothers you, what I do, doesn't it?"

I clenched my hands into fists. "It would bother anyone."

She snorted and dropped her arms to pace in front of me. "Please, don't be so pathetic. Those I use in my sacrifices are weaklings. They do not deserve to live if they cannot resist my power."

I turned on her. "You are a goddess! How can they stand a chance? Your power outrivals even that of your Tuatha De brethren!"

She whipped around, her eyes flashing red, the dark clouds above grumbling their discontent.

"Do you wish to challenge me Caedehn?"

Despite my anger and the slight twinge of fear that burned inside me, I gave a small smile. I stepped back and took on a relaxed stance, crossing my arms loosely over my chest. "You cannot kill me. My geis forbids it."

The Morrigan released a deep breath and pulled her magic back into herself.

"Yes, that little catch has proven inconvenient on many occasions, but alas! Despite your many annoying characteristics, you have proven handy over the years. One of these days you'll outgrow your stubbornness."

"Unlikely," I grunted.

"So," she breathed, dismissing her more somber mood, "besides killing my poor faelah, is there anything else you need to tell me?"

I found a young woman the other day who possesses strong Faelorehn magic.

A Single Thread of Magic

"No," I said flatly, my muscles tensing once again.

She studied my face for a moment or two, her eyes narrowed and her lips pursed as if she suspected something. My heartbeat increased and I willed it to slow down. For a split second she opened her mouth and I was certain she was going to accuse me of lying, but then a flash of crimson lit her eyes and instead she grinned. The expression was very unnerving.

"Very well, you're dismissed." She flapped her arm at me as she turned to leave, the ravens hopping from branch to branch in order to follow her every move while the Cúmorrig trailed after her.

"I shall see you in a month's time, then. Try not to kill so many of my pets if you can help it. You know how much it inconveniences me to perform a creation ritual. And you know how much you enjoy attending them."

I turned and headed back down the dead canyon, punching the trunk of a bleached tree along the way. I would love to kill all of the Morrigan's faelah, but that was the thing: the more I killed, the more she would create. And that meant standing watch as she tortured the living to reanimate the dead. I didn't need any extra horrors to add to my list of troubles.

I spent a glorious week at my castle, just enjoying the free time and the constant caress of Eilé's magic. My last few encounters with the faelah had drained my reserves, and it was nice to feel the pleasant tingle of glamour running through my veins once again.

I would have stayed longer, but my malevolent employer had decided to cook up a whole new batch of particularly annoying faelah that could somehow reproduce on their own. Thankfully, she hadn't insisted upon my presence for the process of their creation, and I had a feeling that they weren't true faelah after all. Eilé had many creatures of magic, some benign and some not. These particular beings, duínba, or

Ebriad

toad people, had a tendency to gravitate towards evil magic. My guess was that the Morrigan had captured an entire colony of them and was manipulating them to bend to her will. It would explain why they were able to procreate. And if I didn't know any better, I'd say she was purposely sending them through the dolmarehn near my home just to bother me. She must have suspected I was hiding something after all.

The duínba were coming through the passageway in such large numbers that I had taken to camping out in the swamp. Even then, hordes of them managed to get past me. By the third night of my stakeout, Fergus and I had killed almost a hundred of them and I hoped we'd finally made a large enough dent in their population to slow them down. For the present, all I could do was grit my teeth and bear it until they stopped pouring through the dolmarehn altogether. I was desperate to get back to my research on Meghan Elam, but it would simply have to wait. If I even took an hour to leave the swamp, the little demons would completely take over. I needed to remain vigilant at least one more night to make sure we'd diminished them for good.

Cúmorrig!

The sudden, frantic thought flaring to life in my mind ripped me from my sleep. My heart pounded against my ribs and I had to take several deep breaths to slow its pace. Was it a nightmare that woke me?

Again, that bright, piercing thought came. *Cúmorrig! Girl in danger!*

I bolted from my sleeping blanket, grateful I had gone to bed fully clothed. It took a while for my sight to adjust to the dark, but I think I managed to move through the forest mostly on instinct. I cut through the trees, running full-out towards my spirit guide, his internal voice leading me on. Something had happened. Something involving the Faelorehn girl and the hounds of the Morrigan. Just a few days ago Fergus and I had been exterminating duínba, and now there were

A Single Thread of Magic

Cúmorrig around? My blood turned to ice when realization hit me. The Morrigan knew about Meghan. Somehow she had found out about the girl and she must know that I knew of her as well. My stomach lurched as I sprinted onward. Had the Morrigan suspected my lie after all?

Yes, my conscience whispered. Oh no, nothing good would ever come out of this . . .

I gritted my teeth and hissed as a long, thin blackberry vine sliced across my neck. I ignored the burn and kept moving. If the Morrigan's hellhounds were involved, then the girl was in real trouble. Could the goddess know what Meghan was, or was she just interested because I had been interested? Or was I simply overreacting? The Cúmorrig could have wandered into the mortal world on their own; it had happened before.

Growling, I picked up my pace, hurdling over a fallen eucalyptus tree and landing in the middle of a small meadow where, it seemed, all hell had broken loose. Off to the side the girl was trying to crawl away from an onslaught of two or three of the hellhounds while Fergus fought off one of his own. I didn't spend much more time studying the scene. With the moonlight to help aid my sight, I reached for the closest Cúmorrig, the one trying to get to the girl's neck.

I quickly took care of the other hounds, breaking their necks and crushing their skulls to ensure they didn't resume their attack, all the while keeping the angry beast that was my fae magic in check. I threw their carcasses deep into the brush where they could disintegrate out of sight. I would be punished for it later; the Morrigan did not appreciate a waste of her favored minions, but at the moment I didn't care.

Silence, like a dark shroud, descended upon the small glade, punctuated only by Fergus's gentle panting.

All clear? I sent him before turning to glance at the girl who was doing her best not to be noticed.

Yes, he returned, *no more faelah.*

Ehriad

Good. Setting my mouth into a firm line, I slowly turned and began studying the young woman sitting on the ground in mute shock. Her face was pale, her eyes wide and her hair a mess. She wore a nightgown of sorts, something that looked more like a long t-shirt. She sat stiffly, obviously terrified, but trying very hard not to let her panic take over. I smiled, impressed with her resolve. Most humans would have lost it by now, after having been attacked by faelah. But she was Faelorehn, made of stronger stuff than your average mortal. However, if I was judging correctly, I'd say she'd never seen anything Otherworldly in her life. But perhaps I was wrong . . .

Taking a small breath, I lowered my eyes, years upon years of training forcing me to study her entire person to make sure she had no obvious injuries. My gaze dropped further and I caught my breath. The nightgown had gathered at her waist, baring her naked legs, pale as her face in the moonlight. For a moment I was blissfully distracted, that is, until my conscience kicked in.

Don't stare Cade. Remember, you want to help the girl, not convince her you are some twisted degenerate . . .

Unfortunately, I think it was too late for that. I could only hope that the hood of my trench coat hid my face from her view. I turned my eyes away, just in case she could see me, though I wouldn't mind studying those shapely legs a bit longer.

Focus Cade, the poor girl's been traumatized. She needs help, not ogling.

While my conscience was busy scolding me into behaving like a gentleman, Meghan decided it was safe enough to talk.

"Who are you?"

Her voice trembled. Time to play it smooth. *You've been dying to learn more about this strange girl for weeks now. Here's your opportunity. Don't mess it up. Slow, careful movements and gentle words . . .*

I dropped into a crouch, trying to make myself smaller so I wouldn't appear so intimidating. Apparently that was the wrong thing to do. She made a small noise and tried to scoot back further, her

A Single Thread of Magic

exposed legs still causing a distraction. I took a breath, ready to say something with every intention to reassure her, but she beat me to it.

"Hobo Bob?"

I could tell right away that she hadn't meant to say those particular words, for she seemed to shrink in on herself and even in the dim moonlight I could see her blush.

"Sorry," she mumbled, scraping at her hair nervously, "I mean-"

I released a small laugh, hoping it would lighten the mood, then spoke before she had a chance to continue, "Is that the title you have awarded me?"

"Huh?"

I chuckled again and stood back up. Crouching was uncomfortable and the fear pouring off of her eased a little when I backed away.

"I often heard the spoken insults of the young people attending your school, but I never paid them much attention."

And it was true. The times I spent loitering around the high school, trying to sniff out faelah and then that thread of glamour she trailed around, I'd allowed my own magic to enhance my hearing and managed to catch several conversations traded between the students. Most of them were tedious, bland or the typical cruel gossip I often found in such places. But on several occasions I'd caught them eyeing me warily and using the moniker 'Hobo Bob' while pointing indiscreetly. I didn't mind. It kept their curiosity at bay. No one ever bothered to pay much attention to a vagrant.

I sighed and lowered my hood. I was through with being Hobo Bob. If I was going to learn more about this girl and in turn help her, then she needed to know I wasn't going to harm her. Though this was not how I planned on introducing myself.

I glanced at her out of the corner of my eye and caught her studying my face. She didn't seem afraid, but almost fascinated. A smug smile pulled at the corners of my mouth and I allowed myself to believe she liked what she saw. Since she was scrutinizing me, I let my gaze drop once again to her legs. Nice legs, long and lean like most of the Faelorehn. I wondered then who she belonged to. She obviously had no idea where she had come from, so I suspected she'd been under the impression she was human for a very long time.

Meghan emitted a small gasp and quickly scrambled to pull her nightgown down. I guess I had been staring a bit too long. I felt my face turn hot and almost laughed out loud. When was the last time I'd flushed like this? Probably not since I was no higher than Fergus's shoulder. Now, why should I care if Meghan caught me admiring her? Oh, this girl was definitely going to cause some turbulence in my already tumultuous life.

"Forgive me," I finally murmured, shrugging off my trench coat and placing it over her shoulders. I hoped it didn't smell too terrible after spending half a week in the woods with me.

"What were those things? Those . . . dogs?" she asked after a long moment.

"Hounds of the Morrigan. Cúmorrig."

"What?"

I huffed a tiny breath. Well, I *had* decided to help her discover who she was, hadn't I?

"Most folklorists would call them hellhounds," I offered. *Yes Cade, break it to her slowly. She's been through a terrible shock.*

We were both silent for a long time and I had a feeling she was either trying to take this all in or simply figuring out how to get away from this nightmare. I couldn't say I blamed her.

"Thanks for helping me, but, um, who are you?"

Not quite what I expected her to say next, but at least she was still talking. I wanted more than anything to spend the rest of the night speaking with her, but what she needed most right now was a good night's rest without any nightmares to trouble her sleep. There was only one way to make that happen and it involved doing something I really didn't want to do.

A Single Thread of Magic

Every Faelorehn being had the power to erase another's memory, but none of us was ever supposed to use that power. Some, like the Morrigan, exploited it whenever it suited them, but others were careful to use it only when necessary, and sometimes it *was* necessary. Like right now. I wanted to help Meghan and in order to do that I had to erase as much of tonight's ordeal from her mind as possible. It would be like erasing the chalk from a board; all one did was smear the white powder around until the words were no longer visible. That's what I'd do with Meghan's memories. I'd smudge them to the point where she couldn't read them anymore.

"You were right in guessing my identity earlier," I said as a way to distract her a little. A distraction always helped with the erasing process.

She leaned her head back to watch me, her expression one of pensiveness. Okay, good . . .

"Our first meeting wasn't supposed to go this way."

Alright, I wasn't really sure how our first meeting would have gone had I had any control over it, but it definitely would not have included the Morrigan's hounds.

Suddenly, she tried to stand up so I reached out a hand and said her name, then blanched. *Not smart, Cade.*

She shied away and murmured something that might have been an expression of gratitude as she tried to hand me my coat. Wonderful. She looked ready to bolt.

"You can't go on your own," I blurted, desperate to salvage what I could from this terrible night.

"Please," she rasped, "I just want to go home."

I stiffened and drew away from her. "You're afraid of me."

Well, of course she is you dolt! Sometimes I really hated my conscience.

It was too late to try to calm her, so I decided to go ahead with my plan. If I was lucky, she'd forget this entire night.

"I screwed this all up, I know, but it's best if you forget any of this ever happened."

She became fully alert, her eyes darting back and forth like a cornered deer.

I moved slowly forward. "Tomorrow, this will all seem like a dream. I'll send Fergus in a week. Follow him and I'll introduce myself properly."

"What are you doing?" she squeaked.

Before she could dart into the forest, I let my glamour flow from my fingertips, enclosing her in an invisible web of magic.

She gasped and started to collapse, but I caught her gently in my arms.

"Who are you?" she murmured blearily.

This time, I answered her.

"You can call me Cade," I said softly, "but you won't remember any of this, so it doesn't matter."

She went completely limp and I scooped her up into my arms, holding her close to my chest. I savored her comfortable weight and breathed in her unique smell for a few moments. The scent of lavender and spring surrounded her and all of my aches and pains from the last several weeks of faelah hunting seemed to disappear.

You could have handled that much better, Fergus said into my mind.

I grumbled and glanced down to find him panting up at me.

Oh, if that isn't the understatement of the evening, I don't know what is, I sent back.

You like her, he returned.

I ignored him and turned to walk up the equestrian path. As we made our way through the dark towards Meghan Elam's house, I could have sworn I heard the echo of canine laughter in my head.

A Single Thread of Magic

The door to Meghan's room was unlocked and wide open. Fergus had admitted to leading her down into the swamp and I had chastised him for it.

You wished to learn more about her and since the duínba were gone I thought it an opportune time.

First of all, we weren't absolutely sure the duínba were all gone, and secondly, don't you think it's a lot more dangerous leading her into a swamp infested with Cúmorrig?

He sniffed and said, *I was unaware of the hellhounds.*

I shook my head. I would never understand canine logic.

Checking to make sure there were no other humans about, I stepped through the door and crossed the room. It was dark, but I could pick out a few details. The room was a bit cluttered and it resembled the typical teenage girl's domain: a lava lamp in one corner, posters adorning the walls, a desk, a small couch, a TV, a computer . . .

I sidestepped a few piles of clothing and came to the bed, laying Meghan's unconscious form gently on the mattress and pulling the sheets up around her. Before I left, I simply watched her for a moment, reaching out a hand and caressing her face. Her skin was smooth and cool and an image of her reaching up and pressing her hand to mine shot through my mind. I pulled my hand back and sucked in a breath. It was dangerous to have such thoughts, especially if the Morrigan knew as much, if not more, than I did. I would have to play this all out very carefully, and if I was smart, I'd assume the goddess knew everything.

Taking a deep breath, I moved away from Meghan and left her to her rest, hoping that I was able to successfully erase those horrible memories form her mind. I slid the glass door into place, trying to be as silent as possible. I lingered for a few more minutes on that small, concrete slab just outside her room, my eyes cast down as I considered the young woman sleeping mere feet away from me.

Fergus's tiny yip snapped me out of my reverie. Against my will, my mouth tugged into a smile as I glanced down at my spirit guide.

Ehriad

His tongue lolled and he gave me that canine grin of his. He didn't have to tell me what he thought this time, for it was apparent in those intelligent brown eyes of his. I released a slow, deep breath as I turned to make my retreat back into the swamp.

"I believe you're right Fergus," I murmured softly as we left the house behind. "I have a feeling this Meghan Elam is going to have a far greater influence on my life than I had previously thought."

The Morrigan's Game

"So, you got my message I see."

I had been making my way to the heart of the Weald, the great forest renowned for its magnitude and magic. Anything could happen amidst these trees, and whenever I entered the realm of the Wildren and the wild forest, I took extra care to keep my ears sharp. And always, my sister managed to sneak up on me without making a sound.

I froze when I heard her voice, the corner of my mouth curving up in a small smile. Enorah made it one of her goals in life to keep the upper hand on me. Shaking my head in amusement, I turned and found her standing on the thick limb of an ancient beech tree, her arms crossed and her longbow strapped across her back.

With agile grace that could only be honed through living in the wilderness, she swung down from her perch, landed lightly on her feet, and strode over to me, her own face graced with a smile. We regarded each other for a moment or two before she flung her arms around me.

"Alright Enorah, let me breathe!"

Enorah stepped back and held me at arm's length.

"Must it always take some disaster to bring you to my forest?"

I arched a brow at her. "*Your* forest?"

She merely shrugged and grinned as if I had no reason to question her.

"The Wild belongs to all of us, dear Caedehn."

"I'm sure Cernunnos would argue that point with you."

Ehriad

She merely snorted and gestured for me to follow her further down the trail. As we walked, she explained to me why she had requested my help.

"I know you are bound to the Morrigan when it comes to dealing with faelah . . ." she said, letting her sentence trail off.

I grimaced. Enorah knew about my geis and the service I owed the goddess.

"But," she continued, "I was hoping you would be able to help me and, more specifically, the Wildren."

Enorah's voice faltered on that last word. The Wildren were the wild children of Eilé; the unwanted boys and girls who ended up in the Weald to fend for themselves. Luckily, they had my sister and a handful of other grown Faelorehn to care for them properly.

I stopped midstride and faced her. "Tell me," I said.

Enorah crossed her arms and took a deep breath, her pale grey eyes flashing towards hazel. "Some strange faelah have made their way into the Weald and have been attacking the children."

I grew suddenly tense, fear lacing my blood. The Morrigan, and her faelah, were not supposed to be able to enter the Weald. That is why the Wildren made it their home. The forest's ancient magic resisted the dark intentions of the goddess and her ilk.

Enorah held up a hand. "So far they have only caused minor injuries, but I don't want to take any chances."

"What do they look like?" I asked, relaxing only enough to keep calm.

"Like nothing any of us has ever seen before. They resemble small alligators, those giant reptiles found in the mortal world. Only these ones have longer legs and necks, and their tails are long and narrow, covered in sharp spines. Their snouts are shorter, but they can still produce a strong bite. It's their tails that are the problem, though."

I glanced up at her. "How do you mean?"

The Morrigan's Game

Enorah grabbed her wrist with one hand, as if she were trying to comfort an injury. "They can wrap their tails around anything, like a noose, and cut deeply into the skin."

I blanched. By the description she had given me, Enorah and the Wildren were being attacked by the Morrigan's latest creation, nathadohr, nasty lizard-like faelah that not only had the barbed tails my sister had mentioned, but a venomous bite as well. The last time I had spoken with the Morrigan, she had boasted about them, claiming they could slip past the magical barrier of protection that kept the Weald safe from her wrath. I gritted my teeth. Looks like she had been telling the truth after all.

"Cade?"

I jerked my head up, Enorah's voice and hand on my arm reminding me where I was.

"Sorry," I murmured, "it seems as if the Morrigan has finally found a way to get to the Wildren. The creatures you described are called nathadohr."

Enorah's expression hardened.

I smiled, despite her fearful look. I knew what she was thinking. Because my geis cursed me to serve the Morrigan, she believed I couldn't attack any of the faelah without her permission. And why would she allow me to kill her monsters if she had finally found a way into the Weald?

"Don't worry. I might have to do the bidding of the Morrigan, but anything she tries to send against the Weald is free game. I can get rid of this little problem without violating my geis."

"Are you sure?" Enorah whispered.

I nodded. "When I was old enough to understand the terms of my geis, I made a deal with her: whatever she created to harm the Wildren, I was allowed to fight without any repercussions. Luckily, she is arrogant enough to think she'll someday be able to create something that can both break through the magical boundary as well as get past me."

Enorah gave me a studied look. "So, how do you plan to destroy them? I don't even know how many of them are out there."

"I do," I said. "There are seventeen of them."

"How do you know that?"

Because I saw the bodies of the seventeen Faelorehn she was able to capture and sacrifice to create them. Yes, I had managed to miss the actual ritual used to create them, but I had still witnessed the aftermath.

"She told me," I said instead.

"How are you going to kill them?"

I dropped my head, gazing at the ground. Hawthorn wood was the most effective way to kill the faelah.

"I know a way, but I'll need your help."

※ ※ ※

The next morning Enorah, several of the older Wildren, and I spread ourselves out along the edge of the Weald, our longbows fitted with hawthorn arrows and several more waiting in the quivers on our backs. Our plan was simple: we would scour the woods for nathadohr and take out as many as we could find.

As we waited I thought about Meghan and our last meeting. After the Cúmorrig attack I let a week pass before sending Fergus, as promised. I waited for her down in the swamp with as much patience as I could muster, all the while listening and looking for any more signs of stray faelah. Fergus and I had spent that week picking off the last of the duínba, but there was always a chance we'd missed one or two.

Eventually, Fergus came trotting around the corner, Meghan's tall, lean figure in tow. The sight of her made me catch my breath. It wasn't so much that she was beautiful, but that the fae magic hidden within her radiated an unseen brilliance, a brilliance that brought every one of my senses to attention. There was no doubt in my mind that she was Otherworldly.

The Morrigan's Game

Reluctantly, I'd left my hiding place behind and introduced myself. She was wary of me at first, but a burning curiosity shone in her eyes and I knew that if I was careful, I could keep her in my presence for just a bit longer. I tried to answer her questions to the best of my ability, but most of her memory of the Cúmorrig attack was gone and in the end, despite my caution, I ended up frightening her anyway.

Realizing that I was sinking fast, I had tried to catch her interest by listing off some characteristics the Faelorehn possessed: the gift to hear the spirits of the earth speaking into our minds, our tendency to have premonitions, our changeable eyes . . . She ended up running away, screaming at me to leave her alone. Fergus's perceptive comments afterwards didn't help improve my mood any. I had ruined this second attempt to make a connection with Meghan Elam. I was quickly running out of chances.

I suppose I could just give up my efforts. It wasn't as if Eilé was devoid of young Faelorehn women, but there was just something about Meghan's innocence that drew me to her. For years I had been able to convince myself that I was happy living on my own, being a loner, being Ehríad. I had depended on no one and no one had depended on me, and I preferred it that way. There were too many ghosts in my past for me to ever live the normal, happy life of an average Faelorehn man. The Morrigan pulled my strings most of the time, as if I was some mindless puppet, and my days consisted of hunting terrifying demons one wouldn't want to meet in their worst nightmares. I had no time for friends, for family, for someone to share my life with.

But Meghan made me reconsider those wonderful possibilities, though I hardly knew her. She made that old yearning, something I had thought I'd destroyed long ago, come back to life like the dying embers of a fire feasting on dry leaves.

I closed my eyes and took a long, deep breath through my nose, picturing Meghan's face: her long, dark brown hair curling down her back. Her beautiful eyes, pale hazel and wide with wonder. I squeezed my eyelids together. *No Cade, not wonder, fear. That night you helped her she was afraid, and again when she met you of her own accord.* I gritted my teeth. I may have completely ruined my last two encounters with Meghan Elam, but I was not ready to give up. When I was done with this job I would go back to the mortal world and find a way to talk to her, but this time I would do it right.

"Cade!"

My sister's sharp hiss snapped me out of my daydream. I glanced up from where I stood behind some bushes to catch sight of her crouching on a tree limb several feet above the ground. She gestured towards the trail with her bow and I squinted my eyes. There, several feet down the path stood a nathadohr, its dark red skin, rough like a newt's and the color of old blood, complimenting the beautiful autumn colors of the forest.

The hideous thing was growling and appeared to be eating some small animal. The nathadohr's teeth were pointed but blunt, and it flicked its long, barbed tail back and forth as it ate. About the size of a beagle and five times as long, the nathadohr shouldn't be too hard to kill. Unfortunately, the muscles that bunched on its hindquarters and front legs suggested otherwise. This creature was very powerful.

Attack?

Fergus's question surprised me. I had forgotten he was with us this morning.

No, I sent, *too dangerous. We'll use arrows.*

Fergus growled in my mind.

I don't want that tail getting you. It has a long reach. Stay put and be ready to go for extra help if we need it.

Fergus backed down and I took another deep breath, drawing the arrow back against my cheek. I took aim for the creature, between the ribs where the heart was. One moment passed and I released the arrow, striking the faelah exactly where I had intended. The thing shrieked in pain, but unlike most faelah that crashed to the ground in agony from the hawthorn wood, it turned and charged me. I froze and

The Morrigan's Game

took note of the smoke, evidence that the wood was in fact working, then darted out of the way as it launched itself at me.

"Cade! Move!"

I threw myself to the ground and rolled as several more arrows sliced through the air. The creature shrieked again as the silent forest filled with the shouts of the Wildren.

Slowly, I stood back up as the archers lowered themselves from trees or stepped out of the brush. Enorah landed next to me with a thud, a fresh arrow ready in her bow.

We moved towards the nathadohr, careful to stay clear of its thrashing tail. Ten arrows protruded from its skin, the wounds smoking as the magic of the hawthorn destroyed it. The creature hissed as it slowly died and I cast Enorah a grim look.

"It takes a lot more to kill them than I had previously thought."

She nodded solemnly.

I huffed a breath and said, "Gather the arrows once it's dead and head back to the village. We might need more help."

For the next few days my sister and I and the twenty oldest Wildren combed the edges of the Weald, searching for nathadohr to kill. After destroying the first one, we learned it was safest if we kept to the trees. During the following week we eliminated thirteen more, but several of Enorah's Wildren ended up with wounds from the tails and venom of the horrible monsters.

The remaining faelah became harder to find and after a day of hunting with no sightings, I began to worry. I wouldn't be surprised if the last three nathadohr had learned how to outsmart us. On the eighth day of our hunt, two small girls were attacked and severely wounded, but we could find no trace of the nathadohr. The girls slept for an entire day, but when they woke they informed us that the three creatures were working together. The memory of the Morrigan's words to me from several weeks ago rose up in my mind like a dark pall of death. Perhaps she had finally found a way to make her faelah more intelligent after all . . .

On the very next morning I woke up early with every intention of finding the monsters on my own. The fog was thick and the forest was silent as Fergus and I left the village behind. Three nathadohr working together posed too much of a danger for Enorah's young wards. Though the Wildren were very capable of defending themselves, they had not been trained as I had.

"Where do you think you're going?"

I stopped in the middle of the trail and sighed.

"Cade, are you leaving us? There are three more nathadohr out there somewhere."

I released a huff of breath and turned to face my big sister, her stubborn face framed by her golden brown hair. For a moment she made me think of Meghan, though the two of them hardly had anything in common. I almost laughed out loud. I didn't know Meghan well enough to know how much she had in common with my sister.

"I'm not abandoning you. I'm going to kill the last three by myself."

Enorah strode forward, her bow in hand and her quiver hanging on her back. She looked ready to hunt despite the early hour and I wondered if she had known my intention to carry on alone.

"No, you're not," she said, brushing past me at a brisk pace. She turned her head and said over her shoulder, "I'm going to help you."

I growled and jogged to catch up with her. "It's too dangerous Enorah."

She snorted out a laugh. "Caedehn! Have you forgotten who I am?"

Her smile was genuine, but there was sadness in her eyes. Her own past was as troubled as mine, but I shrugged my shoulders and moved to join her.

The Morrigan's Game

"No, I guess not," I murmured as we walked silently and briskly down the path.

"Good. We'll find these monsters together and killing them will take half the time it would if you were by yourself. I take it you have a plan?"

I nodded. "Fergus, have you located them yet?"

The white wolfhound stepped out onto the path in front of us like a ghost, pale and silent as the foggy air surrounding us. *Half a mile away, in a cove,* he sent. *Sleeping off a late night hunt.*

"Perfect," I said.

"What?" Enorah asked.

"Fergus will take us there."

Enorah quirked an eyebrow at me.

I simply shrugged and smiled. "The perks of having a spirit guide."

She mumbled something about Faelorehn men and their magical sidekicks before picking up her pace.

Several minutes later we came to a high point on the trail and Fergus trotted off into a small rocky crevasse to the left of us. Enorah and I followed, pushing aside thorn bushes and trying to make as little noise as possible.

Fergus growled and I sent him a quick order to get away from the nathadohr. To my great relief he obeyed, loping past us to wait back on the trail.

They are awake, he sent.

"Get your arrows ready," I told Enorah.

She nodded and the both of us pulled a hawthorn arrow from our quivers and placed them in our bows.

The nathadohr were prepared for our attack, bursting free of the cove like the demons they were. I managed to hit one with my arrow, but it ran past me, whipping its tail around my leg and jerking me to the ground. The spines cut through the fabric of my pants and dug into my skin, making me gasp. The creature was impossibly strong, dragging me several yards before it stopped. It felt like my leg was on fire, but eventually Enorah's shouts of anger cut through the haze of pain.

The monster that had dragged me screamed in agony as Enorah hit it with one arrow after another. Eventually its tail loosened and I struggled to get to my feet. I limped to Enorah's side, pressing my back up against hers as we moved in an awkward circle, searching for the other two nathadohr.

"Are you alright?" I hissed through my teeth, trying to ignore the ache in my leg.

"Yeah, a tail grazed me, but it didn't cut deep."

I nodded, but before I could say anything else another nathadohr burst free from the underbrush, charging us at full speed. It was headed straight for Enorah, so I whipped around, putting myself between the giant reptile and my sister. The nathadohr skidded to a stop, whipping its tail around and dragging the spikes against my abdomen. My shirt tore and the blow left a ragged cut across my stomach. I winced, but kept my arm steady, releasing an arrow and catching the creature in the eye. This time the faelah went down immediately, twitching as the hawthorn burned through its brain.

Enorah cursed and punched me in the arm. "What is wrong with you!? Are you trying to die?"

"No," I gritted, my arm draped across the new wound, "just trying to protect my sis-"

My words were cut short as the tail of the third nathadohr lashed out of the dense fog and managed to wrap around the forearm I wasn't using to guard my injury.

I shouted my anger as the tail tightened, cutting deeper into my arm than the other had done in my leg.

Enorah cursed again, releasing an arrow and quickly going for another. The creature screamed and tightened its tail. I gasped as the barbs cut through flesh and muscle. The agony brought me to my knees.

The Morrigan's Game

"Hang on Cade!" Enorah cried, her voice laced with panic as she kept decorating the nathadohr with arrows.

The monster growled, fighting its imminent death as I fought the blackness that threatened to overwhelm me. Finally, after Enorah had used all her arrows and half of mine, the nathadohr loosened its grip and collapsed to the ground.

When I was absolutely sure that the faelah was dead, I sat up and removed its tail from my arm. I grimaced when I saw the damage, more from its appearance than the pain. The bastard had cut almost all the way to the bone.

"Cade!" Enorah whispered, falling to the ground next to me.

"Are you hurt?" I asked, forgetting my injuries for the time being.

She shook her head. "A few grazes here and there, but nothing serious."

She glanced at my arm and her eyes widened. "Oh no, we need to take care of this."

I nodded my agreement and Enorah helped me to my feet.

It took us twice as long to get back to the village, since I was limping and she was trying to support my weight. When we arrived, several of the Wildren greeted us with a hot breakfast and clean water and herbs to take care of our wounds. We retold our tale over breakfast, and as the fires crackled around us and as the children listened intently, their eyes wide with awe, the pain of the ordeal seemed to lessen.

Eventually I stood up, ready to leave the Weald behind and return to my castle. I was eager to get some rest and return to the mortal world. Now that the nightmare of dealing with the nathador was over, my thoughts concerning Meghan Elam had resurfaced. It had been a few weeks since she ran from me in the swamp, and it was time for me to try and patch things up between us. Again.

Ehriad

"Cade, before you go," Enorah called after me, reaching her arms behind her head and untying a string with a wooden bead attached to it. "Take this."

She tossed it to me and I caught it with my good arm. Arching a brow, I opened my hand and examined the wood. A symbol was burned into it, one that would cast a spell of protection over the person who wore it. I grinned.

"A mistletoe charm? Are you worried about me, dear sister?"

Enorah crossed her arms and snorted. "I'm *always* worried about you Cade. That's what big sisters do."

I smiled, tucking the charm into a pocket.

"I'm sure I'll find a use for it," I said, then grinned once more before leaving my sister and her woodland village behind.

Late morning's broken sunlight shone through the diamond paned window of my room in Luathara, and it took me a few moments after waking up to gather my thoughts. I was in Eilé, not my apartment in the mortal world, and Fergus was curled up on the carpet in front of the fireplace. Late autumn in the Otherworld always promised the kind of cold weather that seeped into your bones, and when I stayed in the castle I needed to keep a fire going at all times. Slowly, I sat up, wincing at the sharp pain in my head and the ache in my arm.

Fergus heard me stirring and sat up abruptly, as if waking from some disturbing dream. He rose to his feet, stretched, then scooped up a piece of parchment that had been lying on the rug in front of him before walking over to me.

"What's this?" I asked, taking the note from his mouth.

I was afraid to read it. It could be from Enorah, informing me that I hadn't rounded up all the nasty faelah encroaching the village in the Weald. Or it could be from my foster father, once again wondering

The Morrigan's Game

why I hadn't visited lately. I could only explain I was too busy so many times. Or it could be from the Morrigan . . .

It is from the mortal world, Fergus sent to me.

I sucked in a breath and with shaking hands, unfolded the letter as quickly as possible. I blamed the tremor on my recent ordeal with the nathadohr, though to be honest, I'd admit it was a result of my anxiety. Before going to the Weald to help my sister with her faelah problem, I had left a note for Meghan, taping it to the sliding glass door of her room where she'd find it. I had wanted to offer my help without frightening her, but I was afraid my first, and second, impression had only made me look worse. So I had written to her, apologizing for everything that had gone wrong and encouraging her to learn what she could about the ancient Celts.

I hoped the letter I held in my hand contained an extension of friendship; Meghan's willingness to give me another chance. I snorted. Yeah, right. Sure, it's what I hoped for, but I wasn't usually that lucky.

My eyes darted over the words, written in a neat, flowing female hand. I smiled warmly. From the little I'd learned from the Faelorehn girl, I could tell this writing reflected her personality well: a young woman with a lot of questions and fear floating around inside her head, but doing her best to remain cool and calm on the outside. My smile only widened when I finished reading it. She wanted to meet with me, after school on Tuesday, and she wanted my help with learning who she was. Maybe my luck was changing after all.

I had no idea when she had left the note in the tree; Fergus must have checked for me while I was napping. It was early Sunday morning, two days before she wanted to meet. I strode over to my desk and took out a quill and some paper, writing a quick note and tucking it into Fergus's collar.

Deliver that straight to Meghan and then come back here and wake me up. We'll be going to the mortal world tomorrow.

Fergus turned and trotted out the door, leaving me alone with my thoughts. I sighed and looked over my shoulder at my bed. I would get as much sleep as possible before leaving for the swamp in the morning. Fighting the nathadohr had almost pushed me over the edge and I could hardly see straight, let alone stand upright. I changed the bandage on my arm, wincing as the gauze pulled away the dried blood, opening the wound again. I applied an ointment and wrapped it up before falling back into bed, anticipating sleep. In the morning I'd head to the mortal world; give myself a day to acclimate to the lack of magic there before meeting with Meghan.

Before drifting off, however, I thought about how I would tell Meghan that she was Faelorehn. A jolt of dread shot through me. How did you tell someone that they were immortal and came from another dimension? Without them suspecting you were crazy? As I finally succumbed to exhaustion, I told myself that this time, whatever it took, I wouldn't terrify the young girl who had taken up a permanent residence in my mind.

Traveling through the dolmarehn of Eilé never took the same toll on me as traveling through the ones leading to the mortal world did. In fact, using the stone passageways in the Otherworld felt just the same as walking through a door and the only way I could tell I had moved from one place to the other was evident in a slight change of temperature or lighting.

I cast my wayward thoughts aside and ignored the discomfort of leaving my world and entering the mortal one. Once I was on the other side, I began hiking down the small culvert and then through the swamp. It took Fergus and I twenty minutes to get to the garage with the small apartment on the second story. It was a little after noon, but I was exhausted. I had an entire day before I'd meet with Meghan and the old lumpy couch would do just fine.

Drawing the blinds and making sure the door was locked, I lay down and threw an arm over my eyes, ignoring the sound of the

The Morrigan's Game

junkyard just next door. Within minutes I was fast asleep, ready to stay that way until late the next morning.

※ ※ ※

Meghan needs help.

The simple statement, coursing through my mind and disrupting my sleep, caused me to snort and sit up. I placed a hand to my forehead and blinked back the sudden headache that always came when waking up with a jolt.

Meghan. She needs your help.

I groaned and turned my face towards Fergus. He was sitting and panting calmly by the couch where I had fallen asleep only a few hours before. No wonder I felt so terrible.

I fell back against the cushions and draped my forearm over my eyes. The rough scrape and sterile smell of my bandage brought back more memories. Ugh, I had meant to change it again before falling asleep. . . I opened an eye. Well, at least the blood stains hadn't worsened. I swallowed, and that act seemed much harder to accomplish than it should have been. My mouth was dry and it felt as if I'd eaten dehydrated faelah the night before. Nice.

What about Meghan? I sent to Fergus, sighing with weariness. I vaguely remembered a note and something about meeting her tomorrow.

She needs help now. Threat.

Sometimes Fergus could sense things before they happened, and for some reason, he was especially sensitive when it came to Meghan. I had asked him about it after he had led her into the swamp that first night, but he couldn't tell me why he picked up on her emotions more than anyone else's.

I groaned and sat up. Now wasn't the time to contemplate my spirit guide's supernatural gifts.

What do you mean, threat? More faelah?

Ebriad

I pulled out the note she had sent me and smoothed the wrinkled paper over my thigh. I was supposed to meet Meghan tomorrow, and I had every intention to respect her need for caution when it came to me, but if she was in danger nothing would stop me from helping her.

No, Fergus panted, pawing at my leg, *enemies at school.*
How do you know? Were you watching over her?
No. Felt magic.

My skin tingled with goose pimples. Magic? Had Meghan somehow used Otherworldly magic? But how? She'd been in this world for a long time, almost her whole life from what I'd gathered, so how could she have any magic to use?

I shook my head and gritted my teeth at the pain it caused. Blindly, I reached for my car keys and grabbed a soda from the fridge, hoping the caffeine would help with my headache.

"Fergus, stay here," I grumbled as I clambered down the steps to the garage.

Very well, he sent, taking my place on the couch and huffing a discontented grunt.

I ignored him and jogged down the stairs, hoping that whatever was bothering Meghan wasn't anything worse than a school bully. In my current shape, I didn't think I could even swat an Otherworldly mosquito without falling over.

🌀 🌀 🌀

The drive to Meghan's school helped wake me up a little, but as I slowed to pull into the parking lot, I caught a glimpse of something that made my blood boil.

Meghan stood on the side of the road, her hands clasping the straps of her backpack as she frantically glanced between the bus schedule and what appeared to be a gang of boys headed in her direction. It was clear she was uneasy, and even more clear that the boys meant to do her harm.

Despite my exhaustion, anger swelled within me, fierce and hot and demanding to take over. *Oh no, not here. I don't need your help here . . .*

I got a hold of my emotions, and my glamour. Instead of turning into the parking lot, I let the Trans Am glide smoothly up to Meghan's side. She didn't notice me at first, far too concerned with the boys who were stalking her.

"Meghan," I said to get her attention.

She turned and saw me, her expression one of surprise. Her heart fluttered in her throat and her eyes flashed with fear, then appreciative relief. I could have smiled, but there were more pressing matters at hand than my wallowing in flattery at her reaction. *Really, Cade, you'd think she was the first girl you've ever interacted with.*

I cast aside my distracting thoughts and leaned across the passenger seat, pushing the door open. "Get in."

Meghan hesitated, perhaps not sure she should trust me. She'd only just met me, after all, and I was a day early. She glanced at the approaching boys one more time before removing her backpack and slipping into the seat next to me.

Over the growl of my car's idling engine and the drone of traffic speeding by on the highway, an angry voice shouted out, "Listen you little slu-"

Before the pathetic whelp could finish his insult, I'd thrown the door open to stand with my back facing traffic, putting the car between me and the vile young man. Oh, if only we were in Eilé and I could use my glamour unhindered . . .

Suddenly wide awake, I growled, "You no longer have any dealings with Meghan. If you ever insult her again, I'll be paying you a special visit at your earliest inconvenience."

It took every ounce of self-control I possessed to keep from digging my fingers into the frame of my car. And at the moment, my glamour was more than willing to lend me the strength to do it.

Ehriad

The idiot must have noticed because he took one look at me, the blood draining from his face, before he turned and marched off, taking his friends with him. My magic fought to take over, but as much as I wanted to tear Meghan's tormentors to shreds, it would not help me win her over in the least. In fact, I'm pretty certain it would be the final nail in my coffin with regards to our current, shaky relationship.

The cars whizzed by on the road behind me, but I merely stood there for several seconds taking deep breaths and willing the anger and its influence on my glamour to dissipate.

When I felt like I had my magic under control, I climbed back into the car and buckled my seatbelt, instructing Meghan to do the same. The tension pouring off of her was strong, but my irritation towards her classmates still lingered. I'd have to work hard not to damage the steering wheel.

I pulled the car back onto the highway with the intention of heading somewhere where we could talk and where I could calm down. Out of the corner of my eye I noticed Meghan studying me, but I only drove on, keeping silent so she wouldn't be alarmed. I wondered what she saw when she looked in my direction. A friend? A potential enemy? The monster that lurked just beneath the surface, the one I was trying very hard not to unleash . . . ?

"Forgive me Meghan," I said finally, "I'm early for our meeting." I took a deep breath through my nose and continued, "And I shouldn't have been so short with you earlier. I wasn't angry at you. I'd just finished work earlier and those young men didn't help improve my mood any."

Okay, so I hadn't *just* finished work but it was part of the reason for my foul mood. Albeit, a very tiny part.

Meghan was quiet for a few moments, then she took a breath and told me not to worry. I wanted to laugh, but I remained still. How could I not worry after what I'd seen in those boys' eyes? And just like that, my anger flared once again. I gripped the steering wheel more

The Morrigan's Game

fiercely and pressed my teeth together, forcing an ache to start in my jaw. *Breathe Cade, breathe . . . Meghan is safe.*

Eventually she asked, "Why were you early?"

Because Fergus sensed that you were in trouble and that you needed my help . . .

Instead I simply shrugged and said, "I had a feeling you were in trouble."

"Something to do with your Otherworldly senses?" she asked quietly.

A chill ran down my spine and my grip on the steering wheel tightened even further. Perhaps she was more perceptive than I had previously thought. Or maybe she had taken my advice and had done a little research . . .

Deciding to play it safe I answered, "You could say that."

We drove for a while longer, turning left at a traffic light and leaving the Mesa behind as we traveled west towards the beach. Meghan asked about our destination and I muttered something about going to Shell Beach. I needed the ocean's soothing presence to help me through what I planned on telling her. From her quiet, tense demeanor I could tell she was preparing herself to ask me some difficult questions. I intended to answer her honestly, and if she was the type to panic then I wanted to be someplace where the control over my glamour wouldn't snap. Meghan Elam was about to learn she wasn't human; that she was immortal and came from a world where gods and goddesses ruled and magic was as much a part of the landscape as the trees and hills. Yes, there was a good chance that she might not take such information well . . .

I glanced over at Meghan to find her gazing out the window, her fingers fretting with the cuffs of her sweatshirt. I allowed my mouth to curve in a smile. In all honesty, I was afraid to tell her the truth; afraid to frighten her. But if I didn't, there would not be a chance to get to know her better and that possibility, more than anything else, was well worth the risk.

Ehriad

I let out a deep sigh as we left the last edges of town behind, driving along a small road that hugged the rugged coast. A few minutes later I pulled my car off to the side of the street and turned off the engine. Meghan took out her cell phone to call home and tell her family that she'd be coming home later than planned. As she spoke I focused on her face. She really was a striking girl, something that wasn't immediately obvious until one studied her further. Her hair, reminding me so much of dark chocolate, curled around her face in soft waves and her skin was smooth and almost too pale, like most of the Faelorehn, but dusted with freckles around her nose. I glanced at her mouth next, her lips curved in a slight smile as she finished up on the phone. Suddenly, I pictured my hand reaching out to her, my fingers running through her soft hair, my mouth pressing gently against hers . . .

"What's wrong?"

Meghan's voice snapped me out of my daydream. What in Eilé was wrong with me? I released a deep sigh, hoping it would take my frustration with it. I really needed to take this attraction I felt and bury it in a deep, dark hole.

I shoved my hands in my pockets and said simply, "Nothing, let's walk."

We made our way down to the beach, taking off our shoes so we could walk barefoot in the rough sand. I closed my eyes and sighed. There were few things in life as blissful as walking barefoot on the beach.

We strolled along for a few minutes, allowing the salt water to soak our feet. Meghan noticed my bandage and I hoped she didn't catch my grimace. I should have changed it again before leaving, but it would have cost me precious time. I had barely made it in time to chase off those boys as it was. I informed her the injury was a result of my occupation, and of course she then asked me about my job.

Well, there is a term for me in Eilé. I'm called Ehríad, a Faelorehn man with no true connections and not the best reputation. It's my job to hunt down renegade faelah and capture or kill them. Oh, and an unfortunate geis binds me to the Morrigan, the Celtic goddess of war and strife.

Sure, that would go over well. Instead I told her some of the truth, admitting that I was a bounty hunter who took care of the Otherworldly creatures that managed to wander from their home. After all, I was trying to break all of this new information to her gently, so I said nothing about the Morrigan or my geis.

Next she asked me about how I had found her.

I detected your magic and followed the trail . . .

"The internet," I said instead.

Someday I'd tell her the truth, but telling her I had been following her around probably wouldn't be in my best interests right now.

Unfortunately, her next question forced me to admit some of the details of the first time I'd seen her.

"But why did you want to learn more about me?"

I paused before beginning my explanation. *Remember Cade, you want to help her discover who she is . . .*

So I told her about Eilé, about the dolmarehn in the heart of the swamp behind her house. I told her that I first noticed her when I detected her glamour along the equestrian path. And finally, after taking a long, deep breath and reminding myself it was the right thing to do, I told her that like me, she was Faelorehn, an immortal being from the Otherworld.

Meghan and I stayed on the beach for a long time. She had taken the initial news of her heritage rather well, I thought, and she spent the rest of the afternoon asking me questions about Eilé. I answered them all, trying to be honest but not too revealing. Part of me wanted to tell her everything but the more responsible part warned me that right now she seemed fine, yet once it all sunk in it might be too much for her to handle.

Just give her a little at a time Cade, just the basic facts. You can fill her in with all the details later, my conscience told me.

This time I took its advice.

By the time we were on the road again the sun had set. We drove in silence, both of us thinking about what had been said today.

As I dropped her off in her driveway, I told her I'd be in touch and that I would instruct Fergus to keep an eye on her.

"Oh, and one more thing," I said.

"What, I'm a long lost princess?" she joked.

I could only smile at that. "No, stay away from the swamp as much as possible."

I tried to keep the ice out of my voice but I may have failed. I closed my eyes tight, thinking about what the Morrigan would do if she knew about Meghan.

I released my breath and said, "The faelah know about you now and I don't know what they might want with you."

Oh, I knew. The Morrigan would be very interested in someone like Meghan, and some of her nasty minions were capable of reporting information back to her. I was obligated by my geis to do the same, but nothing in this world or mine would ever make me betray this strange and wonderful girl.

"Here," I said, reaching into my pocket and pulling out what I found there. It was the small mistletoe charm Enorah had given me after helping her with the nathadohr. She'd probably be horrified if she learned I'd given it away to a girl, but at the moment Meghan needed its protection more than I did.

"Put it on and keep it on your person at all times."

"What is it?"

"Mistletoe," I said with a smile. "It wards against Otherworldly evil."

The Morrigan's Game

She nodded grimly and looped it over her neck, slipping it beneath her shirt to rest against her bare skin. For a delusional second I was jealous of that tiny chunk of wood.

Before I could do or say anything really stupid, I wished her goodbye, telling her that when I got back from the Otherworld I'd teach her how to defend herself against the faelah.

I pulled out of her driveway and headed up the road. As I curved around the first small bend, I glanced up in my rearview mirror. A huge smile broke across my face. Meghan was still standing in the driveway, watching me drive away. *So, she isn't terrified of me anymore. If that's not a good sign, I don't know what is.*

I whistled an Otherworldly tune as I drove back to the garage, feeling confident for the first time in days.

Broken Geis

The sun splayed through the treetops, the spikes of afternoon light driving into my skull like nails. I gritted my teeth and took several deep breaths. Meghan wasn't due for another thirty minutes or so and I desperately needed to spend that time pulling myself together.

I knew what the problem was, even though I didn't want to admit it to myself. I couldn't stop thinking about her. Yes, there was a really good chance that one of her parents was Fomorian, a race the Faelorehn had been enemies with for centuries. Despite what that might entail, I didn't care. Even my foster father had warned me of the repercussions of growing too close to someone who was half-Fae and half-Fomore. I just couldn't imagine Meghan ever causing any harm. But that was only part of the problem. It was who, and what, *I* was as well that made me reconsider growing too close to Meghan.

Fergus whined next to me and I placed my hands on my hips and threw my head back, closing my eyes and letting the afternoon sunlight warm my skin.

"I know Fergus," I whispered, keeping my face aimed towards the canopy above, "but what do I have to offer her?"

If Meghan knew what I was, if she knew what I had witnessed in my long life, our fragile friendship would cease to exist and I would have no chance of hoping for anything more than that. The very thought of not ever seeing her again hurt me more than the raking claws and burning poison of the faelah I often battled.

I had no friends, only a sister, a foster father and a spirit guide. What I would give to have just one friend, to keep Meghan . . . But no, if I truly considered her a friend, if I honestly cared about her, I would tell her I could never see her again. I already feared the Morrigan knew too much and it would be better if Meghan severed all ties with me.

I released a heavy sigh and leaned my back against a eucalyptus tree, thinking about all I had been through in the past week; about the Morrigan's attempt to get information from me. Nausea prickled the back of my throat and my legs felt suddenly weak. As a means of punishment for my insolence, she had forced me to attend another one of her sacrificial ceremonies, and because of my stupid geis all I could do was stand beside her and watch as she brought one victim after another forward, draining them of their glamour and their life force. She had enjoyed every moment of it, absorbing their magic like the parched earth drinking in the first rain of a monsoon. My own anger had burned high and eventually my control failed. The ríastrad, the battle fury that resulted from the volatile mix of my anger and my glamour, burst forth. I had raged for hours, killing as many faelah as I could get my hands on.

The Morrigan had laughed in utter joy, enjoying every minute of it.

"Oh Caedehn!" she had crooned, "Isn't it wonderful? There is nothing like the raw release of violence, now is there?"

I had been sick for days afterwards, and when I met up with Meghan in the swamp a week ago, I was in no shape to visit with her for very long. Not only had I been physically drained of my magic, but the memories of the Morrigan's sacrifice were too fresh. They haunted me even now. Every one of her sacrifices still did and I had witnessed far too many of them. One of these days she would push me too far, test me one time too many. One of these days I would snap and my so-called impertinence would be the least of her worries.

I forced my thoughts to return to the present and ran my hands over my eyes, trying to wipe away the weariness. *Focus Cade. You want your wits about you when it comes time to break off your friendship with Meghan . . .*

But fate would grant me no moment of peace, after all.

"Well, well, well, fancy meeting you here, Caedehn," crooned a familiar voice.

In that moment it felt as if a specter ran its frozen, dead finger up my spine. No. She couldn't be here, not now, not with Meghan's arrival mere minutes away.

I turned, my blood burning with the realization of who had joined me in the meadow. I gritted my teeth as I eyed the woman standing before me.

"What are you doing here?" I hissed.

Yes, speaking to the Morrigan in such a tone was suicidal, but I didn't care. She arched a perfect black eyebrow at me, her fae beauty rivaling the ugliness of her soul.

The Morrigan. The one the Celts called their war goddess. She had owned me for years and I had served her loyally, against my will. She had allowed me to protect my sister and the orphans of the Weald, but that was my only allowance. I could not ask for the protection of Meghan without violating my geis, and that is why I had never once mentioned the lost Faelorehn girl to the goddess. I would not let her get her evil hands on Meghan. But apparently my silence had been all for nothing. Her very next words proved that my suspicions had been right all along: she already knew about the girl I wished to protect.

"That's an interesting young woman you've been trailing after of late. Such raw, untapped magic. And from what I've gathered on my own, she has no clue about it. Do you realize what a rare gift that is my dear Caedehn? A powerful Faelorehn girl, untrained in her magic. She would be like putty in my hands. I could mold her and shape her to my will as easily as one forms clay."

My stomach wouldn't stop churning.

"And I know you've known about her Cade, for many months now. Do you not think I am capable of employing adept spies or discovering such magical gems on my own?"

I would not cringe. It would give too much away.

Broken Geis

The Morrigan released an exasperated breath and studied her fingernails. "So, to answer your original question as to why I am here: to ask you a simple question. Why on Eilé did you not tell me about the little Faelorah the moment you saw her? I don't think I need to remind you that your geis obligates you to inform me of such things, so why did you disobey me and not bring her to the Otherworld?"

I stood still for a long moment, trying to settle my thoughts and come up with an answer to appease the goddess. *Careful Cade,* I told myself as I forced my face into a mask of indifference, *don't make Meghan more of a target than she already is.*

I must have remained silent for too long, because the Morrigan sneered, an expression as familiar to me as my own heartbeat.

"Oh Caedehn, are you pining after this girl? How pathetic! Even if she were worth the trouble, what could she possibly see in you? You are Ehríad, unwanted. You have no titles and no real place in Faelorehn society."

"Don't be absurd," I gritted out. I was used to this, but the last thing I wanted was for her to find out how I felt about Meghan. "I was simply exercising caution. I wanted to make sure she was harmless before introducing her to the Otherworld. For all I know, her magic could blossom and do more damage than good."

The Morrigan threw her head back and laughed, her thick black hair spilling over her shoulders like a dark cloud. The very sight of her made me ill.

"Cade! Do you think you can fool me? Anyway, it's too late. I know she's planning to meet you this afternoon. Why don't we tell her the truth when she gets here? The truth about *us*."

I felt the blood drain from my face. No. It would all be over if she knew the truth . . . Yes, I had decided that cutting Meghan from my life was for the best, but I wanted to do it my way; to let her have at least one nice memory of me. I clenched my teeth and stepped forward, grabbing the Morrigan's upper arm.

Ehriad

"You're leaving. Right now. I don't want you here when Meghan arrives."

"Oh? And why's that Cade? Don't want your little Faelorah to know about the most important woman in your life?"

I froze, my fingers tightening on her arm. She didn't seem to notice.

"Remember, Cade, who gives the orders around here and what happens when they aren't followed."

Her voice was a hiss, her eyes smoldering with the dark red flare of anger and her very own strong glamour. She was holding onto her patience, but only just. I had to get rid of her, but it would cost me.

Taking a deep breath, I loosened my grip slightly and said softly, "If you leave now, I'll owe you a boon."

The Morrigan tilted her head, as if considering, then finally said, "Very well. But I will choose what this favor will be some time in the future."

It was an incredibly unfair offer, but I honestly had no other choice.

"Fine," I bit out, tightening my grip once more as I proceeded to drag her away from the clearing.

I marched her back to the dolmarehn, her arm still clenched in my hand. She strode along with me, not fighting me but continually reminding me of how foolish I was despite the fact that she had received the better end of the deal we'd made. When we finally reached the cave that led to the Otherworld, she jerked her arm free and released a heavy sigh.

"I will return to Eilé for now, but you can't keep this girl hidden forever. I will get my hands on her somehow, and there is nothing you can do about it."

I snorted, though her words scared me to death. Trying to fight fear with false bravery, I retorted, "If that's the case, then you would have taken her by now."

Broken Geis

The Morrigan's face changed, only the slightest inclination of irritation wrinkling her perfect features. *Oh, what's this?* I crossed my arms and adopted a smug look. Might as well keep the act going . . .

"So, why haven't you kidnapped her then?"

The Morrigan sighed and dropped her hands to her hips, rolling her eyes up to the sky. Sometimes she acted like a spoiled heiress and not a powerful queen of Eilé.

"If you must know," she said rather boorishly, "the girl has a geis on her."

I froze, my heartbeat speeding up. If she had a geis, it had been placed on her before she came to the mortal world.

"And what does that geis entail?"

The Morrigan sneered and crossed her arms. "Oh, something about my not being able to touch her. So you see my dear boy, you are worrying for no reason whatsoever. I can't lay a finger on your damsel in distress."

I gritted my teeth. "Just because *you* can't doesn't mean your minions won't. And it doesn't keep you from speaking to her."

The idea of the Morrigan having a chat with Meghan made my skin crawl. The evil woman could convince a fish to abandon its pond to keep from drowning.

She bared her teeth in a grimace, but said nothing for a few moments. She took a step towards the hidden dolmarehn and swept a curtain of tree roots out of her way before glancing over her shoulder at me.

"Oh, have no fear. I have a plan. Enjoy your private time while it lasts. If you have any ideas to thwart me, however, do take into consideration that anything you do to help the poor girl will result in a full breaking of your geis." Her eyes glinted in malicious delight, flashing to red before returning to a violet-gray color. "And you know what the penalty for a broken geis is . . ."

She let her sentence trail off as she disappeared into the dark. A cool breath of air and the thrum of ancient magic told me she was gone, but the chill it brought to my skin wouldn't leave. I didn't want to think about what would happen if I broke my geis, but I had no doubt that sooner than later I'd be suffering the consequences. No, I wouldn't feel those consequences right away, but they would catch up to me eventually.

If I broke my geis to protect Meghan, then I would destroy the powerful spell of magic that came with it. Yes, I had to serve the Morrigan, but every geis came with a price, and the price she had paid when she placed the geis on me had been a spell of protection. As long as my geis remained intact, she could never kill me. If she found a way to hurt Meghan, and I stood in the way, then I basically opened myself up to become the Morrigan's next potential sacrifice. For now I was useful to her, so even if I did do something to help Meghan, I might be safe for a while. I hoped.

I pushed away from the cave entrance and began walking back to the meadow where I was to meet Meghan. Fergus, who had been hiding for the last fifteen minutes, joined me, silent and morose as a lost spirit.

Conflict? He sent.

I squeezed my eyes shut and ground the heels of my hands into their sockets.

You have no idea, I sent back.

I waited another hour for Meghan. I paced for most of that time, anxiety eating away at me like a poison. Why hadn't Meghan shown up? Had the Morrigan lied to me and done something to her?

She's home, in her room, Fergus told me eventually.

I paused, my unease lessening but not disappearing entirely.

Why didn't she meet me? I tried to squash the disappointment, but it bled through regardless.

Broken Geis

Fergus cocked his head in canine confusion. Then he sent me a simple thought: *Sorrow*.

My disappointment fled and I took a slow breath. Why was Meghan upset? Had something happened at school? At home? Had something hurt her? One of the Morrigan's faelah?

"I need to go check on her," I said, almost as an afterthought.

I took a few steps towards the equestrian path, but Fergus whined behind me. I arched a brow at him and he sent, *Asleep*.

I clenched my fists and felt the muscles contract in my neck and shoulders. Every instinct told me to go check on Meghan; to protect her. But if she was sleeping then she was safe, for now.

"Alright, I want you to stand guard at her door and make sure nothing tries to harm her. I'm going back to Eilé. I have a feeling that I'm going to need the full power of my glamour very soon."

Fergus's sharp barks woke me from a dead sleep. I bolted upright out of bed, a searing, white-hot pain crackling through my brain.

I pressed a hand against my forehead, gasping in slight shock.

"Fergus!" I growled as I climbed out of bed.

I grabbed a pair of pants and pulled them on but didn't bother with a shirt. My skin was still hot from the fever that often plagued me after using my magic to its full extent.

"Why didn't you send me an unspoken message?" I demanded of my spirit guide, now yipping and scratching at the bedroom door.

I did. You would not respond. Too deep in sleep.

I contemplated his silent words and lowered my hand. *So why this need to wake me? How long have I been asleep?*

Many days. Meghan is in trouble. The Morrigan has lured her into the Otherworld.

Ehriad

I cursed, bringing the sharp pain in my head back to a nearly unbearable level. Pushing the discomfort aside, I frantically began to pull on my shoes. How could I have been out that long without waking? And how could Fergus fail to reach me? He'd always been able to reach me. It's as if I'd been drugged . . .

I froze, but just long enough to feel the cool rush of dread coursing through me. Of course. The Morrigan had done something to keep me asleep for so long. I don't know how, but I was certain of it. She knew that I would do whatever I could to help Meghan. She knew I would break my geis. Which meant she also knew what Meghan meant to me . . .

"Where are they Fergus?" I asked as I tore through the door, taking the steps down into the great entrance hall two at a time.

The stone circle, just on this side of the dolmarehn leading into the mortal world.

I took a deep breath and broke into a full run. As soon as I made it over the bridge and into the fields, I called out for Speirling, my stallion, using the same method I used to speak with Fergus.

The black horse must have sensed my urgency because he trotted up a few minutes after my call.

"To the wooded hills Speirling, as fast as you can!" I shouted as I nudged him towards the west.

We flew across the fields, Fergus close on our heels. The wind cooled my hot skin but it did nothing to calm my agitation. I was so angry, but worry and terror dominated every other emotion. If the Morrigan got what she wanted before I arrived, Meghan might not live to see another day.

I urged Speirling up the narrow path between the hills, risking the chance that he might trip and injure both of us. When he couldn't make it any further because of the thick brush and rough terrain, I leapt

Broken Geis

from his back and hit the ground running. I cut across the thick woods, leaving the trail behind, and headed directly towards the dolmarehn. I would most likely have several new bruises and scratches from the times I ran into branches and tripped over rocks, but a more direct route would get me there in half the time. My exhaustion pulled at me and my breath came in quick pants, but I pushed myself ever forward, hoping beyond hope that Meghan was still alive.

I burst through a final thicket of dead bushes and stumbled upon a horrible scene. The fog was thicker here, brought on by the Morrigan's magic. I darted my eyes around, taking in the image of the goddess in her battle garb: a black dress that mimicked a dark cloud of evil. Various faelah, all of them rather small, gathered around the stone circle, half-covered in the earth they had just emerged from. The chant filling the air was a familiar one; one I had heard many times at the Morrigan's rituals of sacrifice.

Suddenly, a sharp cry drew my attention downward. Every last nerve in my body went numb. There, lying on the damp ground and pressed up against one of the tall stones was Meghan, covered in blood and surrounded by almost a dozen of the Morrigan's hellhounds.

"Meghan! *No!*"

I didn't even try to fight my magic as it surged forth, taking only a few moments to overwhelm me. I had been through this process recently, and it wasn't safe to go into my battle fury again so soon, but Meghan's life depended on it. My unique gift, the strange power my glamour gave me, something I had inherited from my father, rippled over my skin and for a few agonizing seconds, I was trapped in a world of pain. When the agony stopped, I blinked a few times and glanced at Meghan. I couldn't tell if she was still conscious; I couldn't tell if she was still alive. Pure, raw fury took control. I eyed the closest Cúmorrig, still trying to tear her apart, and roared, a sound that was more animal than anything else.

In my current state the Morrigan's hounds were easy to kill. I grabbed one after another, tearing them apart with my bare hands or throwing them against the stones circling the entrance to the dolmarehn. At some point in time, the Morrigan fled in her raven form, but I ignored her. I killed one hellhound after another, and when they were all destroyed I turned to the faelah that had arrived to take part in the massacre. I can't say how long I fought them, but when there were none left my battle fury slowly dissipated and I almost collapsed to the ground.

My head was pounding and my muscles felt like they'd been through a shredder. I fell to my knees and squeezed my eyes shut until some of the pain went away. I took several deep breaths, my heart rate slowing with each one.

A tiny sound drew my attention away from my own personal ordeal and I looked up to see Meghan. My heart nearly stopped. She was covered in several lacerations and purple bruises were forming all over her exposed skin. She coughed once, a horrible wet sound, as if she was choking on her own blood.

I scrambled over to her side and, as carefully as I could, scooped her up into my arms.

"Meghan!" I rasped, "Oh no, stay with me darling girl!"

She felt so frail and I cursed myself for failing her. I ran my hand through her tangled hair and leaned close to whisper in her ear. I spoke to her in the language of Eilé, a spell of magic often spoken over children when they were sick. I poured my heart into that spell and willed the magic to keep her with me. My lips touched her temple. I hadn't meant them to, though there was nothing I wanted more at the moment. Ignoring the small voice telling me that Meghan needed far more than kissing right now, I continued pressing my lips to her skin, making a trail down to her mouth.

Her eyes fluttered and closed and just before she lost consciousness and went limp in my arms, I pressed my lips to hers, giving in to what I had desired for so long. But it was too late to enjoy it; to learn if she felt the same way about me. The kiss lasted a split second before I cried out in fear.

Broken Geis

I pulled away, still holding her, and shook her shoulders gently. "Meghan? Meghan!"

Take her back to her world. To a hospital. Her family will worry and she will be frightened if she wakes up here.

Fergus's voice in my head jerked my attention away from Meghan.

I growled and clenched my teeth. I didn't want to take her to a hospital. I wanted to keep holding her and whispering words of magic over her until she healed. But Fergus was right. I was certain the magic of Eilé would take care of what the Morrigan and her ilk had done, but this place was so foreign to her that it might be too overwhelming, at least for the time being. The mortal world did, after all, have its own magic. Not nearly as powerful or as pure as Eilé's, but magic nonetheless. And being Faelorehn, Meghan was stronger than most.

Wise old hound. I don't like it, but you're right. It's what's best for Meghan.

Fergus trotted up to me, his tongue lolling. He had a few cuts from the fight, but most of the blood staining his pale coat looked like the rotten blood of the faelah.

I scooped Meghan's unconscious form up as I stood, cradling her against my bare chest. I didn't mind the cold, and I liked how Meghan felt pressed against my skin. I would much prefer to have her awake and returning the gesture, however. I entered the dolmarehn sideways so that we would fit, and in the next breath the magic swept us away.

We arrived in the mortal world moments later. The Trans Am was in the garage on the other side of the highway, but I needed it to get Meghan to the hospital. Carrying her would be a bad idea. It was after dark already and if anyone saw me carrying an injured girl, both of us covered in blood, I'd have too many uncomfortable questions to answer. I sighed and looked down at Fergus.

I need you to guard her while I run and get the car, I sent to him.

Ehríad

Fergus panted and pulled his lip back in a half snarl. *I'll kill anything that comes near her and cloak her in glamour if the Morrigan arrives.*

I nodded once, my face grim, and gently lay Meghan down in a bed of leaves. I placed my hand against her face and leaned in to kiss her one more time. Her lips were soft and warm, something that surprised me considering the shock she had been through. I wanted to let that kiss linger, but I'd already taken advantage of her once and I needed to get her to safety as quickly as possible.

I'll be quick, I sent to Fergus, then took off jogging down the trail. As I ran, I kept the memory of kissing Meghan close at hand. I wondered if she'd remember it when she woke up and what she would think of me. The warmth of that thought quickly died as I remembered the Morrigan's words to me: "You are Ehríad. Unwanted."

A bitter dose of pain twisted my heart and I pushed myself harder. I should not let the Morrigan's thoughts affect me, but some things were not so easy to dismiss. Besides, thinking of my conversation with the Morrigan reminded me that I had done what I had avoided doing for so very long: I had broken my geis. I had interfered where I had been told explicitly not to.

Oh well, I thought with a sigh, *water under the bridge. I'll deal with the consequences when they come my way.*

Within twenty minutes I was walking back up the dirt trail to my car, cradling Meghan in my arms. She was still unconscious, but breathing steadily.

When I carried her into the emergency room at the local hospital, the staff reacted immediately, taking her behind closed doors to tend to her injuries. The clerk at the counter asked me what had happened, eyeing my bare and bloody torso, so I made up a story about a pack of coyotes and how I just happened to be driving by. I gave the woman a fake name and the moment she glanced down at her paper to add it to the report, I used a bit of my glamour (what little I had left) to slip out of the door unnoticed and to make her forget what I looked like. I wanted more than anything to be by Meghan's side, but a

Broken Geis

hospital was no place for an immortal Faelorehn. Well, at least not one who was unfamiliar with the ways of the mortal world. She would be alright, I knew she would. She had strong magic in her and it would help her recover. I would simply wait until she returned home to speak with her.

I drove out of the hospital parking lot, scowling at the orange glow of street lamps as I headed back for the Mesa. Yes, Meghan would heal and she was safe. For now. I gripped the steering wheel of my car, my knuckles turning white. Meghan was safe, but I wasn't. The Morrigan would not take my interference lightly, and I knew this time my punishment for disobedience would be much worse than it had ever been. This time she might actually kill me, as she promised.

I returned to Luathara to lie low and allow myself to heal. An entire day went by and I did nothing but sleep. Fergus watched over me, coming and going between my castle and the mortal world as I had instructed him before I fell asleep. In my dreams he let me know how Meghan was doing, and as long as she was safe I managed to stay put.

When I finally woke up late in the evening I felt a little stronger, but I knew better than to think I was well enough to take up my old duties. Secretly, I hoped the Morrigan had forgotten I'd broken my geis or that she'd find me too useful to destroy. I snorted. I sounded pathetic, even to myself. But it wasn't out of fear for my own wellbeing that concerned me, it was out of fear for Meghan's. Despite what I had told her regarding the world she had come from, she really had no idea what she had stumbled upon that fateful night in the swamp. And after spending more than a lifetime alone, enslaved by an evil goddess, I wasn't ready to give up what little happiness I might have found. No, I didn't fear death or suffering, I feared losing Meghan. I had been willing to forget her, to walk away for her sake. But after all that had happened, I knew that option was no longer possible. As long as she lived and as long as I did as well, I knew I'd be forever drawn to her and forever compelled to protect her. In order to do that, I had to remain close to her, or at least as close as I could.

Sighing, I ran my fingers through my hair and scrubbed the sleep from my eyes. I glanced across the room, taking in the moonlight streaming through the window. Just after midnight. I'd get up and take a shower, then Fergus and I would make a little trip into the mortal world. Meghan should be home from the hospital by now and although I was still feeling rather ill myself, seeing her awake and breathing would be a balm to my spirit.

The moon was low on the horizon when I stepped free of Luathara's courtyard, my breath misting in the chilly air. Dawn was still a few hours away, but Speirling would get me to the dolmarehn long before the sun rose. I lifted my head and drew breath to whistle for him, but the lone, dark outline of a figure several yards away gave me pause.

I recognized that silhouette, the same one that had been the bane of my existence for all my life. The Morrigan. So, she had come to claim my life after all, or perhaps the unnamed boon I had promised her. Very well. If she wanted my life, I would fight her. I would most certainly fail, for as weak as she was after her attack on Meghan, I was even weaker.

I dropped my arms and spread them, as if to offer up my soul.

"Come to collect what is owed to you? Don't expect me to just hand over my life. I'll fight until the end."

The Morrigan moved forward, like fog drifting over the land, until she was only ten feet away from me. She crossed her arms and turned up her nose. There were dark circles under her eyes and she looked paler than normal. Killing her Cúmorrig and interrupting her

Broken Geis

sacrificial ritual must have taken a far greater toll than I had thought. I tried to hide my smirk of satisfaction.

"No, Caedehn," she sighed, sounding grossly disappointed. "You are far more useful to me alive than dead for the time being. Oh, but you will regret what you did."

I huffed out a breath of frustration. I had wondered if she would prolong my suffering and I guess I had been right. I pushed by her, the sensation of prickling ice running up my skin where I had brushed her arm.

"Well, if you aren't going to kill me then I'll be on my way. I have something I need to do."

I wasn't about to tell her where I was going, but of course, she already knew.

"You can't protect her, you know. And now she's more vulnerable than ever before."

I stopped and turned around, my hands clenched into fists. "What do you mean?"

"Her geis. She broke hers as well. As long as she stayed in the mortal world she was immune to me and my faelah. Now she's as helpless as an infant all because I convinced her to follow me here."

No. She was lying. Meghan wouldn't have followed her; she wouldn't have entered the Otherworld with someone she didn't know. But why *had* she come to Eilé?

"I don't believe you," I snapped. "You've sent your faelah after her before." Meghan had told me as much.

The Morrigan snorted. "Yes, and none of them have ever been able to harm her. I even tried once but only met with a powerful shield of magic. Someone placed a geis on her when she was very young, a powerful geis."

I swallowed, my throat dry.

"Who?" I croaked.

The Morrigan's lip curled wickedly. "Do you really think I'd tell you Caedehn? You are lucky I am allowing you to continue

- 69 -

breathing. But mark my words, I'll be getting what is due to me, all in good time. Just not today. I want to play with you and your little Faelorah for a little bit longer."

I shook with anger. I didn't know what was worse, knowing that I now must await my death, or knowing that she would make what was left of my life miserable.

"Until then, you will work twice as hard as before."

"No, my geis is forfeit. If you wish to kill me, do so now. I won't give you another moment of my life."

She no longer had the power to control me and if she wanted a slave, then she would have to find someone else. Or kill me.

She sighed heavily and shifted her weight, as if the burden of the world was placed on her shoulders.

"You do owe me a boon, if you recall, and the threat of death is obviously not going to work on you. So, I have an alternative."

She stepped forward, her power rising all around her, weakened from the recent fight but still present. Still dangerous.

"If you do not do as you're told, I will kill your precious fae strayling where she sleeps. I will draw it out, make her suffer, and you will be there to witness it. And then I will do the same to you. Do not anger me beyond my limit Caedehn, for as you well know, I am not in the least bit the forgiving sort."

"Very well," I gritted out, "what do you want from me?"

"Meet me tomorrow morning outside my fortress and I will give you instructions. Now," she said, taking a breath and clapping her hands together, "do run along to the mortal world and check on our common interest. You won't be seeing her for quite a while and I want to make sure you know what you'll be losing should you decide to betray me again."

With a flash of dark magic, the goddess transformed into a huge raven and took to the skies, croaking in avian laughter. Only when her cawing faded into the distant east and I knew for certain she wouldn't be hunting Meghan today, did I turn back to the fields.

Broken Geis

Speirling arrived a short time later, an inky blotch against a sky of the same color. Fergus soon joined us, reappearing after the Morrigan had left. He had a habit of making himself scarce when she was around.

A half an hour later I was picking my way through the dark hillside, climbing to the spot where Meghan had almost died. I shivered as I approached the dolmarehn, the damp, dark earth still reeking of death and evil. Taking a deep breath, I passed through the stone gateway and came out into the shallow swamp behind her home. I had done my best not to think about all that had passed in the last few days; of what horrible things the future might hold.

Think only of the fact that you are alive, that Meghan is alive, and as long as you are both breathing, there is a chance to defeat the Morrigan.

I snorted at my own absurd thoughts, but as I crested the small slope behind Meghan's backyard, I tried only to think of what I would say to her and wondered if she would ever forgive me for not giving her more warning with regards to the Celtic goddess who so desperately wanted to destroy her.

Meghan slept peacefully in bed, her figure very still in the dark. One leg was free of the covers, the one the Cúmorrig had broken. The cast made it look swollen. I clenched my teeth and fought a swell of anger. Before I could so much as punch the wall, Meghan stirred and turned her head towards the door. I froze, not sure if I wanted her to see me yet. I allowed a small trickle of glamour to help me blend further into the darkness. Even that little bit made my head pound.

She threw back the covers and sat up, but then paused. Had she seen me? I couldn't tell. Sighing, I called my glamour back. *Time to stop hiding, Cade.*

Meghan tensed and then scrambled to get back under the covers. I grinned beneath my hooded jacket. So, she hadn't seen me . . .

Ehriad

I waited a bit longer, to let her decide whether she wanted to invite me inside or not. A small nod of her head informed me that I was welcome. With my heart beating erratically, I reached out and nudged the lock with a little more glamour, then gently slid the door open. Once inside, I removed my trench coat and set it to the side. When I got close enough to see Meghan's bruised face and cut skin, I heard her make a small sound of distress. I froze.

"Oh Cade," she murmured, reaching out.

Instinctively, I flinched away, then immediately regretted it. Had I not dreamt about this? Had I not longed for Meghan's touch?

"I'm sorry Meghan," I whispered. "This is all my fault."

I glanced at her broken leg and then pulled up a chair and practically fell into it. I was so weary I could hardly stand.

"I should have told you so much more," I murmured, more to myself it seemed than to Meghan. "You never should have crossed into the Otherworld."

And then I told her, all that I could. At some point, she tried to comfort me again, but I wouldn't let her. I had nearly caused her death, all because of my fear and stubbornness. But I couldn't erase the compassion in her eyes and I did allow myself to enjoy her concern if only for a moment.

I told her that I had been learning what I could about her heritage and that an old friend had been doing some research for me. I couldn't tell her anything more than that since I hadn't had a chance to really discuss his findings with him yet (I'd been pretty tied up with my own problems for the past several weeks), and that he wasn't an old acquaintance but my foster father. He had assured me that what he had found proved Meghan was far more important than I could have imagined, and right now she didn't need that extra shock added on to everything else she'd been through. But she tried to get it out of me anyway.

"Your geis," Meghan said quietly. "You can't tell me because it will violate your geis."

Broken Geis

I opened my mouth to deny that claim, but paused. Lying to her was a very bad idea, especially since I wanted her to trust me. But a small lie now wouldn't hurt.

"Yes," I said, "in a way. I violated my own geis just recently and one of my punishments is to keep certain information to myself."

She seemed to deflate in front of me and I hated myself for misleading her. *But you will be safer now Meghan, for not knowing, and I don't even know the details myself. Let's deal with your recovery, and then we can hunt down your family tree.*

To my great relief, she recovered quickly and then asked me about my own broken geis. Blanching at the memory of that terrible night, I admitted I had broken my geis by saving her life. I also told her about how the Morrigan wanted her dead and how she had wanted me to deliver her to the goddess.

Meghan's shock didn't surprise me in the least, so I continued on, undeterred. "She distracted me with an assignment in the Otherworld and I hate myself for not being there to help you."

Okay, that wasn't a complete lie. It wasn't an assignment that had tied me up, but the fact that I was trying to recover from using my ríastrad at one of her rituals. But there was no way I was going to tell Meghan that. She didn't need to hear about any more death and suffering and I was too afraid she would shut me out forever if she knew what I did in my free time.

"So, tell me more about my geis," she prompted after clearing her throat.

I drew in a sharp breath, then let it out slowly. *Here goes . . .*

In so many words, I informed her that her geis had been a magical shield, protecting her from the faelah so long as she never set foot in the Otherworld. When I was through with my explanation I held my breath, waiting for her anger. But she never got angry. She simply sat calmly, nodding her head ever so slightly.

"That's why they could never really hurt me. And that's why the Morrigan didn't harm me in the clearing in the swamp. Because she couldn't."

She glanced up at me, her beautiful, changeable eyes wide with realization. "That's why she told me you needed my help, to lure me into the Otherworld . . ."

I flinched and she stopped speaking. There was plenty to focus on in what she had been saying, but of course all I heard was that she had gone to Eilé for one reason.

"Help me?" I asked, not truly believing it.

Her cheeks turned pink and she glanced away, muttering something that could have been an acknowledgment to my question.

I smiled, but didn't allow it to grow too wide. We were, after all, speaking about broken geasa and the wickedness of a wrathful Celtic goddess. No longer able to stop myself, I reached out and took her hand. It felt warm in my own icy one, so I brushed my thumb against her skin, reveling in the sensation and trying to communicate my appreciation of her act.

"Thank you," I whispered, my voice slightly hoarse.

Meghan took a deep breath and said, "I bet your girlfriend is really ticked off. That was you who I saw in the Otherworld the other night, right?"

Every muscle in my body contracted, including the ones in my hands.

Meghan gave a soft cry and tried to tell me that I was hurting her, but I had temporarily lost the ability to process simple thoughts.

"Girlfriend?" I rasped, my stomach roiling with revulsion.

Meghan nodded. With some effort, I relaxed my grip on her hand.

"The Morrigan is *not* my girlfriend. Is that what she told you?"
"No, I just thought-"
But she didn't finish her statement. She didn't need to.

Broken Geis

"She would want you to think that." Oh yes, that was just like her, to confuse Meghan and use her emotions against her. I shuddered, partially in disgust, partially in irritation.

"I assumed, well, after seeing the two of you in the woods-"

She bit back the rest of that sentence and retreated into herself again.

"You saw us in the woods?"

Oh no, what had she heard? A new wash of fear flooded over me. Had we discussed anything that might give Meghan the wrong impression? Well, worse than the impression she already had? I tried to think of what was said, but my brain was just too tired to recall my memories.

Eventually, I looked back over at her and searched her face. No, she hadn't heard much. Thank goodness.

"Meghan, the Morrigan is definitely *not* my girlfriend."

I suppressed a horrified shudder and remembered that soon I would have a new set of grueling tasks to keep me busy, and to keep the Morrigan away from Meghan.

"I have to go soon Meghan," I said after awhile. "I have a broken geis to make up for."

"Will I ever see you again?" she asked softly, not meeting my eyes.

I will do everything in my power to make sure that happens.

"Perhaps, when I've done my penance," was all I said.

Then I remembered the torque I had bought in Kellston so many weeks ago, still tucked away in my trench coat pocket. I had seen it while passing through the small town and I had instantly pictured it perched around Meghan's throat. A woven band of silver with two hounds' heads growling at one another. I had purchased it without a second thought. Now would be the perfect time to give it to her.

"I have something for you," I said, reaching my arm behind my back and conjuring the torque from my coat pocket several feet away.

Ehriad

The moment the cool metal found my fingers, I drew it forward and presented it to Meghan.

"What is it?" she asked.

"A torque. The Celts wore them into battle. It will help protect you while I'm gone."

Meghan went very still and fresh tears began to spill from her eyes. I sucked in a breath and cast aside all my careful restraint. I reached out a hand and placed it against her cheek, catching the tears as they fell. I wanted so badly to lean in and kiss them away; to kiss away her pain. But I held back.

"Meghan, listen to me," I whispered, my voice raw, "you are stronger and much more powerful than you think, but I'll leave Fergus here to look after you."

She blinked up at me, fighting the tears as she tried her best to be brave. "Can't I come with you?"

Oh my darling, how I wish you could . . . I smiled, and I knew it was more an expression of sadness than joy. "No. Your fae power awoke when you came to Eilé, but it is very weak."

I explained to her that although the Otherworld would feed her power, it would take a long time and I still needed to teach her how to use it. And I wouldn't be able to do that, not right away. It was safer to stay in the mortal world for the time being.

"Thank you for the torque," she said eventually.

I grinned. "It suits you."

The morning approaches, Fergus sent, jerking my attention away from Meghan. *If you wish to be rested when you meet with the Morrigan, you should return to Luathara now. I will look after Meghan.*

Thank you Fergus, I sent back.

I glanced back down at Meghan, studying every detail from her mass of dark hair, slightly disheveled from sleep, to her hazel eyes flashing from green, to gray and back again, to her small nose peppered with freckles. I would hold that image in my mind as the Morrigan gave me tasks I knew would tear away a little bit of my soul, one day after

Broken Geis

another. No, I wouldn't succumb. I would hold Meghan's image close and that alone would keep my spirit intact. It would have to.

I stood and turned to leave, but Meghan's voice, quiet and pleading, stopped me.

"Cade?"

I turned my head and gazed at her.

"Be careful. And come back soon."

Tilting my head ever so slightly, I answered, "I promise."

Before any other words could be exchanged, I turned back around, stepped through the sliding glass door, and disappeared into the grey light of early dawn. Fergus followed after me, only to see me to the dolmarehn. I had meant what I'd said to Meghan; that he would stay behind. She needed him far more than I did and besides, he wouldn't set a single toenail within a mile of the Morrigan if he could help it.

Dead eucalyptus leaves crunched under my feet and the gloomy fog dripped its discontent upon me as I made my way to the gateway of my world. My every nerve was drawn tight and my hands shook, not only because of the rest I so desperately needed, but also because of the raw emotion that coursed through me.

For now I would serve the Morrigan, as much as it horrified me just to think about it. If that was what it took to keep Meghan safe, then it was worth the sacrifice. And when I could extract myself from the goddess's talons, if she didn't kill me first, I would discover a way to bring Meghan to Eilé, and I would find a way to earn her affection and convince her to become a permanent presence in my life. I would find a way to overcome everything that separated us.

The next several weeks of my life would be hell, but if it meant seeing Meghan again, healthy and whole at the end of those weeks, then it was worth it. I would survive the Morrigan's wrath, and when she was through with me I would do whatever it took to win Meghan Elam's heart.

Acknowledgments

For this particular book, I want to especially thank all of my readers. I can't express enough how much I appreciate your support, encouragement and kind suggestions with regards to the scenes you wished to read from Cade's point of view. I only hope that these three short stories live up to your expectations.

About The Author

Jenna Elizabeth Johnson grew up and still resides on the Central Coast of California, the very location that has become the set of her novel, Faelorehn, and the inspiration for her other series, The Legend of Oescienne.

Miss Johnson has a degree in Art Practice with an emphasis in Celtic Studies from the University of California at Berkeley. She now draws much of her insight from the myths and legends of ancient Ireland to help set the theme for her books.

Besides writing and drawing, Miss Johnson enjoys reading, gardening, camping and hiking. In her free time (the time not dedicated to writing), she also practices the art of long sword combat and traditional archery.

For contact information, visit the author's website at:
www.jennaelizabethjohnson.com

Books by This Author:

The Legend of Oescienne Series
The Finding (Book One)
The Beginning (Book Two)
The Awakening (Book Three)
Tales of Oescienne - A Short Story Collection

The Otherworld Trilogy
Faelorehn (Book One)
Dolmarehn (Book Two)
Luathara (Book Three)
Ehríad – A Novella of the Otherworld